*The Second*
*Vanetti Affair*

*By Marc Lovell*

THE SECOND VANETTI AFFAIR
THE BLIND HYPNOTIST
DREAMERS IN A HAUNTED HOUSE
AN ENQUIRY INTO THE EXISTENCE OF VAMPIRES
A PRESENCE IN THE HOUSE
THE IMITATION THIEVES
THE GHOST OF MEGAN

# The Second Vanetti Affair

MARC LOVELL

PUBLISHED FOR THE CRIME CLUB BY

DOUBLEDAY & COMPANY, INC.

GARDEN CITY, NEW YORK

1977

All of the characters in this book
are fictitious, and any resemblance
to actual persons, living or dead,
is purely coincidental.

Library of Congress Cataloging in Publication Data

Lovell, Marc.
The second Vanetti affair.

I. Title.
PZ4.L89913Se3 [PR6062.O853]    823
ISBN 0-385-12828-2
Library of Congress Catalog Card Number 76–50778

*First Edition*

# Foreword

In a previous novel, *The Blind Hypnotist,* ex-vaudevillian Jason Galt, down on his luck, dreamed up a way of bringing himself the celebrity he craved. He would kidnap a famous person, using hypnotism for the capture, and then render him void of memory. The hope was that when, after every ounce of publicity had been milked from the disappearance, Jason returned the victim to freedom, he would have eradicated the past from his mind. He would be assumed an amnesiac. As he would not respond to normal treatment, only the voice of his hypnotic control, the man would remain in this state—until Jason came forward to offer assistance. He would "cure" and attain instant fame.

The one he settled on was Elsie Vanetti, an actress. At thirty-two, she was internationally famous, had recently won an Oscar, was presently appearing in a London theatre.

After two failures at the stage door, Jason found Elsie there alone. He put her into a light trance and took her to his flat.

While headlines round the world blared, and Elsie's husband, small-time actor Hull Rainer, was showered with attention plus offers of work, Jason used all his talent in making Elsie recall every incident from her past and then ordering her to expunge it from her mind. He also, without being aware of it, fell in love with his victim. He began to feel guilt at what he was doing; began to think of using the benefits not for personal glory but to further the fledgling science of hypnotism.

At last Elsie was ready. Jason took her to Covent Garden

and brought her awake. He had told her that all she would remember was an impression, one of wandering.

Elsie was found, treated in hospital and then moved to a psychiatric clinic. No one could find a cure for her amnesia. Jason telephoned Hull Rainer and offered help. Eventually, he was given the go-ahead.

Elsie was now back home. Jason spent a day with her. He told her that later, when she got the signal, she would remember everything up to leaving the theatre. Then he began to talk, covering her whole life.

That night, Jason, Rainer and Elsie went to the stage door. It was there that Jason would "cure" her; and she was wearing the clothes she had worn before. This would mean good publicity for Jason. It would also mean the same for Hull Rainer, and was the reason he had let the hypnotist help. Hull had felt the loss now that the headlines had died away.

With police and press waiting along the alley, Jason positioned Elsie by the door and then hid himself. He gave the signal. Elsie came out of her trance. She began to revile Hull Rainer and charge him with being an adulterer. She was tired of it. She had decided that tonight it would end. Her manner had the quietness of controlled hysteria. Finally she drew a letter-opener from her purse and tried to stab her husband.

As he rushed forward to hold Elsie, Jason realised that the only way to keep her from going through with her intentions was to put her back, forever, in the nonmemory state. He didn't care about Hull Rainer, but Elsie's life would be ruined if she killed him. So Jason sent Elsie into a trance, returned her to the amnesia of minutes before. She was safe now, but Jason's scheme was ruined, for he would have to say he had failed.

# The Second
# Vanetti Affair

Elsie Vanetti was two months old. Today was an anniversary, a milestone. Although her body was thirty-two years of age, only sixty days had passed since Elsie's mind had been born, slapped into life by the bustle and racket and stench of Covent Garden.

She smiled. She felt proud of herself, felt the anniversary as an achievement. That she had come through the fear and strangeness of those first weeks was amazing. She would never have believed it possible.

But she was anxious no longer. And no longer did she have the suspicion that the whole thing was a weird conspiracy. She was calm, perhaps contented.

Certainly there was the constant thrill of discovery. Every day Elsie found out something new about herself. She liked the colour blue above all others. She loved tea, cold toast, any kind of pasta, an aperitif sherry, walking in Hyde Park across the way, the children's programmes on television, misty evenings, warmth. The list was long.

Her dislikes were not so numerous, which pleased her, for this hinted that possibly she was a nice person. The factor yet to be discovered was her personality.

She loathed cold showers and boiled potatoes and beer. Noise she hated. She disliked fast traffic, the smell of fish, the touch of marble. She disliked the woman she knew to be her mother, which was sad.

Experiencing a twinge of guilt, Elsie strolled into the living room. It was large, bright, pleasant. There were four chrome-and-leather couches around a low table.

Elsie went to one of the windows. She stood looking out with arms folded under her ample breasts.

Elsie Vanetti's face was handsome. It had a firm jawline and a serene brow. A slight Roman curve took her nose out of the Anglo-Saxon commonplace and matched the wide mouth. Her eyes were large, dark, compelling. She had blond hair that fell in gentle waves from a centre parting to nuzzle her shoulders and neck.

This September evening, Elsie wore a triple outfit in pale-blue wool: skirt, top, cardigan. She had bought it herself on the first shopping trip of her new life, when she had been as thrilled as had appeared to be the crowd of women who followed her through the store.

Looking out at the traffic below on Bayswater Road, with dusk blurring the park's great trees, Elsie thought apropos of personality that although it was bad of her to dislike her mother, surely it was good she was able to feel guilt about it. She dismissed the question. Similar ones plagued her a dozen times a day.

Elsie went back to her list of dislikes, hoping she had come to the end.

There was Hull, she mused. With him it was not a matter of dislike. He had treated her well, had been courteous. Yet he always seemed to be tense in her company. He made her feel uncomfortable. And surely emotion didn't disappear with memory. Surely after seven years of marriage there'd be some rapport.

Elsie shrugged. It didn't matter any more. The problem of having a stranger for a husband was solving itself.

When Elsie had returned here from the stage door, after Jason Galt's unsuccessful attempt to cure her amnesia, she had found the apartment empty. Hull didn't come home that night. Next afternoon he telephoned to say he was staying with friends. He added, "Could I come over and get a few things?"

Puzzled, Elsie said, "Why, of course. Naturally."

Half an hour later, she and Hull were sitting in the living

room, facing each other across the centre table. Hull was pale. His clothing and hair lacked their usual perfection. While speaking, he kept his gaze mostly on the carpet.

Elsie asked, "How long will you be away, Hull? Is it to do with an acting job?"

His voice was low, quietly harsh. "Listen. The truth is, I won't be coming back."

"Oh."

"The truth is," he said, again, "I'm going ahead with what we decided before you disappeared."

Elsie shook her head. "I'm sorry, I don't understand you."

"Separation," he said, glancing up. "A divorce, in time. You don't remember, of course, but we talked it all out long ago. I was just waiting to find a suitable flat."

Elsie felt nothing. Her sole concern was reflected in the question, "What was wrong with our marriage, Hull?"

He flipped his hands up from his knees. "Lots of things."

"Was it me? Was I at fault?"

"We both were. Marriage in show business is tricky at the best of times. We tried hard. We were fond of each other—we still are—but we just couldn't get along."

Elsie leaned back. She said, "I'm sorry."

"So am I. Can't be helped. One of those things."

"Is it final? Does everyone know?"

"It's pretty final, Elsie, but we haven't told anyone. We can keep it that way for the time being, if you like."

"I don't suppose it matters, but all right."

There was little to say after that. Hull packed a suitcase and left. He said he would get the rest of his things when he was settled.

Elsie had not been lonely. Friends called often. The char who came in three mornings a week was a cheerful, garrulous woman. There were cooking and shopping and household chores. And there was Jason.

Smiling, Elsie left the window and began to stroll around the room. It was curious, she thought that she knew more about Jason Galt than she did about herself.

The hypnotist was the person Elsie had seen most during the past two months. Every day he telephoned, every other day he stopped by, every third or fourth day they went out together. Elsie felt secure with Jason. It was as if she had known him for years, but she realised this was not so. He seemed to understand her, understand everything. He had shown no surprise on learning that Hull had left.

Elsie was still smiling as it occurred to her how good it was to have so many points to add to her list of likes. She liked Jason's walk, his strong hands, the sound of his voice, his involvement in his work.

There was only one dislike, Elsie mused. Jason had a quietness, a reticence, which seemed to be due to sorrow, or regret, or remorse. Perhaps there was a woman behind it all.

Elsie brightened. She told herself Jason's manner could be because of his failure at the stage door. It hadn't helped that the reporters had sniggered, or that the next day's press reports of the attempt had been brief and derisive.

Unconscious of the act, Elsie lifted her chin. *She* believed in Jason's talent. What was more, she had proof of it. Already he'd helped her to remember several incidents from her past, though, oddly, nothing from the previous seven or eight years. But that would come in time. Every meeting with Jason filled in another blank patch.

Leaving the living room, Elsie went into the kitchen. She put on the kettle for coffee. As she cut a slice of apple pie her thoughts, still in connection with Jason, went to the play they had seen together the night before.

She had loved it. Even though it had been an awful production with second-rate dialogue and a virulent case of miscasting, she had adored every minute. She loved theatre. She had seen twenty plays and was hungry for more. A great one left her limp with satisfaction, like an athlete after victory; a poor one sent her ego soaring, like a wealthy widow in a brothel. But it was fine just to be in an auditorium before curtain-up. The sight and smell of the place, the murmur of talk and the feel of expectancy, these were enough to send her pulses racing.

Elsie had long since accepted that she was a famous actress, which at first, despite being shown her pictures under blaring headlines and seeing herself in a newly released Hollywood epic, had seemed absurd. Acceptance of this had made her able to believe all the other, more mundane facets of her forgotten self, hastening serenity.

She had been convinced of her profession not only by her love of theatre, which a fan could have, but by her knowledge of the craft. She might not know where her husband kept his shirts, but she knew how a particular stage effect worked. She might not have heard of people called Ibsen, Shakespeare, Shaw, Osborne, but found she could quote their works at length. She might be unsure of her maiden name, but was glib with all the esoteric cant words of the acting trade.

She was an actress, glad and proud of it, and looked forward to the time when she could return to work.

Elsie took her coffee and pie into the living room. She sat on a couch and, while snacking, glanced through one of the dozen scripts stacked on the table. These had been sent by producers, even the one of her last play, which, without Elsie Vanetti, had been forced to close.

In two or three months, Elsie thought, with full readjustment, she might be ready to pick up where the amnesia had left her off.

She was still reading fifteen minutes later when she heard a key in the flat door. Taking the script with her, she went along a passage and into her bedroom, leaving the door open.

A male voice called, "Hi. It's me."

Elsie answered, "Okay." She sat on her bed and went on reading.

Three days before, Hull Rainer had telephoned. He was having his new flat painted, he said, and would appreciate it if Elsie would let him move into the guest room until the work was finished—a week at most. Elsie had agreed.

Hull had been no trouble. He left early and returned late.

They had ignored each other politely. In fact, Elsie had hardly been aware of her husband's stay.

She wondered now, however, letting the script droop, if this was Hull's way of attempting a reconciliation. She found she had no fondness for the idea. Her life had fallen into a comforting routine. She had nothing against Hull particularly, but felt for him no emotional response. It must be true, she had reasoned, that love had died in their marriage. If Hull made overtures . . .

Elsie shook her head at what might never be and went back to reading.

Presently the doorbell rang. Before Elsie could move, she heard Hull call, "I'll get it." Next came the sound of the flat door being opened. Eyes roaming aimlessly, Elsie waited to find out if the caller was for her. Half a minute went by.

The next noise she heard was a thud. It sounded like something heavy falling in the carpeted hall.

Elsie called, "Who is it, Hull?"

There was no answer. She found herself listening intently. She called again: "Hull?" Still no answer. Elsie put the script aside.

When the man appeared she gasped. It was the abruptness of his being there in the doorway which had startled her. Immediately she gasped again. This was for the horror that was the man's face.

Under a dirty slouch hat, above a high muffler, was an eerie brown mass of wrinkles, twists and flattened features. The eyes were hardly visible. A depression formed the mouth. The ears were flat, as if glued to the head.

A fire victim, Elsie thought. Regretting her reaction, she tried to erase it with a smile. It came on as a weak flicker. She was shaken. She had run through three different emotions in almost as many seconds.

Now came another shock. The man was holding a gun.

Elsie clasped her hands and stared. The first thought—that this was Hull playing a joke—went as she realised the man was taller and much heavier than her husband. He wore a blue boilersuit and knee-high rubber boots.

Elsie next realised she had been mistaken about the face. It was not covered with scar tissue. The man was wearing a nylon stocking over his head.

Confused, dizzy, her heart thudding, Elsie stammered, "What . . . what . . ."

The man spoke. "Keep nice and still, dearie," he said. His voice was gruff, its accent Cockney. He hadn't moved from the doorway. He stood with feet spread and the revolver aimed.

Elsie jerked out, "Where's Hull?"

"The husband?" the man said. "Don't you fret about him. He's sleeping nice and peaceful."

"What've you done to him?"

"A little tap on the head, dearie. Be as good as gold in a while."

Elsie was recovering her presence of mind, though her heart still overworked and there were aches of weakness in her knees. Involuntarily she glanced toward the telephone.

Under the nylon stocking moved a ripple that might have been a smile. The man said, "It's dead, your extension. I took the receiver off in the lounge."

Elsie drew a deep breath, clasped her hands tighter. She asked, "What d'you want? Money? There isn't much in the house. I only have a few pounds. I—"

The man was shaking his head.

Elsie said, truthfully, "My jewellery isn't here, except for a couple of rings. It was put in the bank weeks ago. We don't have a safe here." Because the stranger was shaking his head again, she added, "It's true. Believe me."

"I do, dearie. It's not your sugar I'm after."

"Then what do you want?"

That ripple came under the nylon. "You," the man said.

A maniac or a rapist or both—that was Elsie's thought. She told herself she had to react with care, to treat the man delicately, humouringly. But she was startled to hear herself blurt:

"If you touch me I'll scream!"

The man said, "Go ahead. These flats're soundproof. Posh stuff. Insulated walls, double windows. Scream all you like, dearie. And if it gets on my nerves, I'll kill you."

She believed him. He spoke so casually. He might have been threatening a slap in the face. That made his words more vicious than if they'd been snarled.

"To put it another way," the man said. "You'd best keep your mouth shut."

"Yes," Elsie whispered. She looked down as the stranger began to move forward. Rounding her shoulders, putting the clasped hands between her knees, she tried to make herself smaller.

The man stopped three feet away. She could see the rubber boots and the bulky boilersuit legs. A shudder ran over her. It was due more to revulsion than fear.

She wondered if she were going to fight; if, in fact, that was the kind of person she was. She thought not and hoped not. She had no wish to risk being shot.

The man ordered, "Stand up, dearie."

Elsie slowly got to her feet. She kept her gaze down. It met the gun. She quickly looked aside.

"Listen to me," the man said. His voice had become low and urgent. "Are you listening?"

Meekly: "Yes."

"You and me's going for a walk. Out of this flat and away from here. I'll be right beside you. Try anything, and I shoot. Is that clear?"

Elsie nodded as well as saying, "Yes."

So it couldn't be rape, she thought. The man was mad. Or, hopefully, he would keep her out of the way while partners came in and stripped the flat. There were some valuable furnishings.

"Get a coat."

Elsie moved over to the closets that covered one wall. She

opened one and took out a topcoat in navy-blue tweed. Putting it on, she fastened the four large buttons.

She looked toward the man, looked not directly at him but in his area. In answer to a gesture from the gun hand, she went forward, heading for the bedroom door.

The stranger fell into place at her back. She felt the muzzle of the gun prod into her spine and stay there.

They went along the passage and into the hall. Off it opened a guest bedroom. The door was open. Lying halfway through, face down, was her husband.

She made an unplanned move to turn aside, to give aid. The gun jabbed, the man said, "Forget it, dearie. He's all right."

Elsie came back into line. She murmured, "Poor Hull."

"Only a little tap. Now be quiet. Okay?"

"Yes," she said.

"Open the door. Be careful. See if the corridor's clear."

Elsie drew the door open. She looked out. There was no one to be seen. She said, "Clear." The gun jabbed. She obeyed, passing outside and turning right. She heard the door close. With the man close behind she went along past the elevator and toward the service stairs.

---

Hull Rainer got up shakily. His hands were trembling. He went in three fast strides to the apartment door. The first time he tried to open it, the catch slipped from his fingers. He tried again, succeeded.

He stepped outside. The corridor was deserted. At a semi-run Hull went to the right. He passed the elevator, which was silent, and reached the door leading to the service stairs.

In the door's upper half was a small window. Hull looked through. He saw in gloom only the bleak stairwell, nothing human. He opened the door and listened.

From below came the clump and tap of feet on the stone steps. The sound was descending.

Hull slipped through the gap, let the door close softly

behind him. Moving to the rail he peered over. He saw a blue-clad arm, recognised the tweed material.

About to go down, Hull stopped when his shoes tapped loudly on the first step. Stooping, he swiftly removed his casual slip-ons and thrust them in the pockets of his blazer.

Quietly he began to descend. His hands were still trembling and muscles near his eyes twitched at regular intervals.

He passed the door to the floor below. Sounds of descent were still floating up. The next door he came to was that leading to the lobby. Through it, he could hear people talking: two of the women residents. Hull went on.

He could feel the cold of the stone through his stockings, feel on his palm the grain of the wooden bannister rail, smell the dampness of the stairwell. These realities were no help. He still seemed to be dreaming.

From below came a creak and then a thud. The sound of footsteps chopped off. Hull hurried on down. He came to a dead end in which was the last door. He looked through its window into the basement garage of the apartment building.

Nearby was a small van, grey, splashed with mud on the bottom part. The box body had no windows. The back doors were open. Elsie was climbing inside, head down.

Trembling, Hull watched.

When Elsie had gone from view inside the van, the man quickly closed and locked the doors. He put his gun in a pocket of the boilersuit. With a swift movement he lifted aside his hat with one hand while with the other he pulled off the nylon stocking. He went to the driver's door, opened it and tossed hat and nylon in.

He turned. He looked at Hull Rainer. He nodded. Hull nodded back.

The man got behind the steering wheel and slammed the door. Hull turned away and started to run up the stairs. He went in huddled caution past the lobby, was careless about the next floor, stopped at the other to put on his shoes.

From what he could see of the corridor through the small

window, it was deserted. He went through. All clear. Running
again, Hull went to the apartment, inside and closed the door.

He looked with bright, keen eyes at his hands. They still
trembled. Hull grinned. He had never guessed there would be
a bonus in this—excitement. That the unsteadiness might be
due to fear he quickly dismissed.

Hull strode into the living room and went to a cocktail cabinet. He poured a whisky. The glass he put down again after
half raising it. Suddenly he had started to laugh.

Head lolling, he weaved over to one of the couches and let
himself flop. He laughed helplessly. He laughed until the tears
pooled between his cheek and the leather. He laughed with
closed eyes and gaping mouth, like a crier. He laughed himself weak and calm.

Hull sat up slowly. He sighed, wiped his face, looked at his
hands. They were steady. But, he thought, inside he still felt
great. It was thrilling, all of it, the act and the plan.

The plan especially. It was brilliant, beautiful and safe.
*Safe.* So Elsie decides to play awkward? Or she manages to
break away? Or she attracts a neighbour's attention? Or she
evades Dave long enough to dial the police?

Hull Rainer, actor, rose from the couch. He slipped into an
open-armed pose and said with a light, earnest smile, "Darling. Elsie, it's me. I'm here. Don't worry. You're perfectly
safe. Be cool, darling. There's nothing to get upset about."

Hull gestured to one side. "Dave, take that stocking off, for
God's sake. There, see? It's old David Reece. I believe
you two met years ago. Oh, but of course, you don't remember. Well, Dave's a friend. Please try and calm yourself,
darling.

"What? My idea of a joke? Oh no, Elsie, of course not. How
could I do anything like that? If you could recall me from before, you'd know I'm not the type. Listen. Let me explain.
Come sit down here beside me."

Hull lowered himself back onto the couch, one arm
stretched out along its top. His smile had gone but his

earnestness had increased. Hull was enjoying himself immensely.

Gentle, he said, "I, with Dave's kind assistance, did this to try and help you. It's been two months now, Elsie, and there's been no change for the better. True enough, you and I are going to get divorced, but I'm still terribly fond of you, as I'm sure you must be aware. I always will be. So I wanted to do what I could to help."

A brief smile, a pat of invisible hand, and, "I did this for two reasons. First, acting. If you thought you were in danger from an armed man, you would start planning how to get away. To do so, you'd have to put on a performance of some kind—pretend to be ill, do something to distract his attention, get him to believe whatever story you could think up on the spur of the moment. You see, darling? You'd have to act, and be damned good to convince a gangster. Your old self could. It would be marvellous for you to know your new self could as well."

Hull nodded, lapsing from his role. The story and its presentation were great, he thought. He almost felt sorry they wouldn't be needed.

Acting again, earnest, he said, "Secondly, there's your amnesia. I thought that as everything else has failed—doctors, shrinks, hypnotism—there'd be no harm in trying shock. You know, jolt your memory back. Ah, well. Too bad it didn't work. And after all the time I spent working on it."

Hull pushed a pout, which quickly went, as he smiled on reflecting that at that juncture it would have been his turn for sympathy and petting. Yes, it was too bad the story wouldn't be needed.

Hull lay back on the couch, sprawling his legs and arms. He rested his head and smiled quietly at the ceiling.

Albert Green, who took the classier name of Hull Rainer in drama school, was attractive in a pretty-boy way which was no longer fashionable in the acting profession. That was the reason he got so little work. The reason he got what he did get, that was because of his famous wife.

Hull had a smooth, round face, an upturned nose, sensual lips and expressive eyes. The cut of his black wavy hair was as outmoded as his features; a lock fell cutely onto his brow and helped the kid image he aimed for. He was thirty-two and hated it.

Of average height, Hull was well-formed because he had spent years doing regular bodybuilding exercises. This pertained above the waist. A mirror-athlete, his legs were skinny. He had a facial twice a week, plucked grey hairs from his temples, took care of his diet, smoked and drank in moderation. He fawned upon himself.

His clothing style had, again, nothing to do with current trends. He always set a tone somewhere between rising actor and college graduate. He now wore a check shirt open about a scarf, a blazer with silver coins for buttons, and sharply creased flannels.

The happiest days of Hull Rainer's life had been during his wife's recent disappearance. No longer obscure, his name was known to millions, to everyone who could read a newspaper or listen to the radio, and his face became familiar to the millions more who had time only for television.

Reporters had trailed him. People had pointed him out in the street. A tabloid had paid him a lavish sum for the right to ghost his autobiography. With ease, his agent was able to line up a part in a movie and the lead in a projected TV series. An advertising agency was keen to use him for sponsorships.

Almost as wonderful as this attention and promise was the ease with which he had been able to pick up his short-term mistresses. Not that he had ever found the hunt difficult, but now it was like shooting sitting birds. It had been simply a matter of selecting the preferred type: pretty, shapely, worshipping, and, above all, young.

Hull had not realised the depth of his happiness at the time. This was normal. Like most people, Hull needed, in the first place, the yardstick of aftermath comparison, and, in the second place, he was unwilling to admit that at other times his life was less than perfect.

Now Hull got up from the couch. His action had the limb-loose indolence of a self-satisfied child. He sauntered into the hall, where he began again to act, his body slumping to suggest bewilderment, his face projecting worry and contained anger.

"So I called out to my wife I'd answer it, Officer," he said. "She was in the bedroom. I opened the door and there was this man. I thought at first it was a gag. That lasted only a couple of seconds. I knew as soon as he spoke he meant business. He said for me to turn around. I did, and then I felt this terrific pain in the back of my head. I blacked out."

Hull wondered if the investigating officer would be the same as in the Vanetti Affair, that bastard Wilkinson. Hull hoped so. Last time, blue-ribbon pig Chief Inspector Harold Wilkinson of Scotland Yard had as good as accused him of being behind Elsie's disappearance, the charming suggestions ranging as far as murder.

It would be great, Hull thought on, to have Wilkinson and side-kick Detective-Sergeant Bart on the job, they this time sure he was innocent and he knowing bloody well he wasn't.

After enjoying that reflection for a moment, Hull went back to his rehearsal. He said:

"Well, Officer, there's not much I can give you in the way of description, I'm afraid. You've seen a face under a stocking. See one, see them all. For the rest, he wore a fedora, gloves, a blue boilersuit and wellingtons. That's all. Build? Well, fairly heavy and about six foot."

Hull assured himself it would be quite safe to say that height, give a couple more inches than the seeming actual, which had been built up from the true actual of five-seven by false heels in the overlarge boots (it had had its uses, his knowledge of the tricks of the acting game, though the extra clothing under the boilersuit had been Dave's idea).

Exaggeration of height would be safe because it would never do for his description to tally too closely with Elsie's. That would be dangerous, for it was notorious that witnesses rarely agreed.

"Anyway, Officer, next thing I knew I was lying on the floor, right there. I had a god-awful pain behind my right ear. It was like a hangover. In fact, I thought I'd been drunk and passed out. I got up. I was weak and dazed. I went and poured myself a whisky."

Hull walked into the living room and over to the cocktail cabinet. He picked up his drink, sipped, put the glass down.

"It was only then I remembered this man. Burglar, I thought. But I was still feeling too awful to look around. I finished the whisky before I checked the desk—that's the only place we keep papers and a bit of cash. Nothing had been touched. Then I became dizzier from the pain. I felt behind my ear."

Hull picked up the glass and drained it with one draught. His face was nonacting grave as he turned away. Now came the part he dreaded. Hull had a loathing of all physical violence.

He went to the guest bedroom, where he had been sleeping —with the door locked against a return of memory to his murderous wife. The bed was an antique four-poster. With the awkward movements of nervousness, Hull sat on the floor with his back to one side of the bedfoot, sat on his rump and with legs outstretched.

Shuffling, he moved into position. The post was immediately behind him. One of its bulbous sections touched the back of his head in the spot he wanted: he had worked out the position previously.

Hull's face had paled and become unsteady. He took a tight grip on his thighs. Every muscle was tense. He drew a deep, deep breath, closed his eyes, nodded low—and then slammed his head back.

At the pain and the noise, and the fear of both, Hull cried out. It was a high-pitched cry that was itself frightening. But the fact of having actually done what he must, yet had doubted being able to, this gave him the courage to slam his head back again. His voice and the pain shrieked.

He was going to vomit. He jumped up and ran to the bathroom and teetered over the bowl. Nothing came. The feeling of nausea faded. Furthermore, the pain was slackening. As Hull straightened, there were tears in his eyes. Pride.

Arranging the side flaps of the mirror, he was able to watch his fingers probing the injured spot behind his ear. He pressed coaxingly on the outskirts. The pain came now only when he got too brave. He continued pressing until he succeeded in drawing blood.

His bladder tickled. His relief was great that the two hits would suffice. He watched the blood gather for a trickle; watched until, after reaching and darkening his shirt, the red line became still, its source drying.

He went back to the living room and sat down to recuperate from his ordeal.

The exorcising of Hull Rainer's possession by happiness, that had begun at the stage door. At first he failed to notice the ebb. He was too relieved to be alive, to have escaped Elsie's knife. At a friend's house he cuddled the fact of his safety, shuddered through recollections of the near-stabbing, and dwelled on the shock of Elsie having found out about his girls; more, of her seeking them out and hearing from them his fetish of abusing them verbally when his loins were sated.

Recovered from relief, fear and shock, Hull discovered that the Vanetti Affair had gone the way of all ephemeral flesh. It was unmentioned in the media, untalked of in the streets. The exorcism came to a rapid, successful conclusion. Hull Rainer was ignored. The advertising agency lost interest, the TV series fell through, his part in the proposed motion picture was given to someone else. Hull was frustrated and angry. Not only had he no work, but as he and Elsie were breaking up, there was no prospect of the roles which would normally go to "Mr. Vanetti."

It was while in this state of depression, future bleak, that Hull saw the grand design which would give him back the lost glory.

Hull rose from the couch. He lit a cigarette and strolled metaphorically onstage.

"No no, Officer," he said. "It's nothing. Really. I looked at it in the bathroom mirror. I shan't need a doctor. I have a pretty strong skull, y'know.

"Anyway, when I got over the dizziness, I looked around the apartment. My wife wasn't in her room. I took another look around and finished up in Elsie's room again. That's when I saw it."

Hull walked offstage as he left the lounge and went along a passage. He came into the bedroom he had formally shared with his wife.

Taking out the handkerchief which protruded too much from his breast pocket, Hull stepped to the vanity table. His eyes chose from among the chaos of cosmetics the lipstick he would use; his linen-draped forefinger and thumb picked it up.

Across the mirror he wrote WE HAVE ELSIE VANNETI! WE WILL BE IN TOUCH BY POST ABOUT THE RANSOM. CODE: XYZ.

Hull put down the lipstick and stepped back, the artist. He liked the appearance of the message. The wording he was already fond of (particularly the misspelling of his wife's surname) and had spent many happy hours getting it just so and even practicing on bits of paper, which he had afterwards burned.

Humming cheerily, he headed for the living room to pour himself a small snort of whisky. The stage was set.

Hull's grand design was for Elsie to be kidnapped. It would have more drama potential than a mere disappearance. Vanetti Affair II would blaze across the media of the world. Hull's star would once more be in the ascendancy.

It had been fun working out mechanics. The hardest part had been recruiting the chosen partner, David Reece. Hull had gone three times out to Reece's farm before getting an agreement. Never had he been forced to work so hard at selling.

Reece gave in only when assured of total security, plus, of course, the one thousand pounds assistance fee. Repeatedly Hull had ticked off the safety measures.

One: Hull would be present for the abduction and give his

covering story if anything went wrong. Two: Reece would not need to put on his stocking mask until in the flat. Three: Hull would go to the farm every afternoon both to spell guard duty and let Reece go into the village, where he was seen at that time daily. Four: They would say, if the whole thing fell apart halfway through, that Elsie had been in on it as well, for the publicity.

David Reece had been left without an argument.

Hull intended playing to the script of safety, save in respect of number Four. He would let Reece make his claim of collusion, and then deny it with outrage. He would say everything had happened exactly as he had first reported it, and admit only to a vague aquaintanceship with the kidnapper. Anything other than that would be his artistic ruin, quite apart from the criminal aspect. Elsie, of course, would make the same denial. It would be their word against Reece's. He wouldn't have a hope.

Hull finished his drink, looked at his wristwatch. It was twenty minutes since David Reece and Elsie had left. By now they would be two thirds of the way to Apple Acres farm.

Hull went to the telephone to call the police.

———◆———

The record player was spinning at 78 rpm. The turntable had no record, the pickup arm was set aside. Instead, a small flashlight, switched on, twirled in the centre.

The girl was sitting three feet away, in a low and comfortable chair, her head level with the record player on the desk. Her face pulsed with the on-off glow from the spinning flashlight.

"It's fascinating, isn't it?" Jason Galt said. "It's soothing. It creates an optical illusion of a continuous band of light. Concentrate on it and you will see what I mean."

The girl nodded slowly. "Yes." She was in her late teens and wore a cheap cloth coat. The prettiness of her young hands was marred by gnawed fingernails, some all but invisible, one hidden under sticking plaster, two bloody from recent chewing.

At a deliberate speed in his deep, caressing voice, Jason Galt said, "I think you will agree that it is like the feeling of approaching sleep. Sleep. When you are feeling sleepy. Tired. When you are longing for sleep."

Staring at the twirling light, the girl sighed. Jason smiled. The subject's attention was held and her motor output restricted. It was going to be an easy one.

He said, "Sleep. It is like sleep. When you are aching for sleep. So tired, so sleepy, so drowsy that you can hardly keep your eyes open. Don't you agree?"

The girl murmured an affirmative. She let her head droop back on the chair. Her blue-painted eyelids looked heavy, swollen.

After more repetitious talk, Jason crooned, "You are longing for lovely sleep. It would be so wonderful if you could rest. And you can. I am going to let you. Would you like that?"

The girl, face immobile, whispered, "Yes."

"Close your eyes."

She obeyed, lowering her eyelids slowly. She was in a light hypnotic trance.

Reaching over, Jason stopped the turntable and switched off the flash. He leaned back with folded arms. As always, even though it might happen a dozen times a day, he got the feeling which vaguely embarrassed him, the feeling of power.

The hypnotist was tall and slim. At thirty-seven he still had the vitality of youth because of that weight lack. His shoulders were broad and rounded, defensive. He had large hands. The tweed sports coat, business shirt and plain slacks, each garment rumpled, seemed to have found their way onto the wrong person, like fleas on a god. Jason Galt had the kind of presence, a theatrical grandness, which called for a cloak, or white tie and tails, or at least a dashing uniform.

When, a minute ago, Jason had smiled, his face had looked charming and kind, even innocent. Now, in repose, it was the picture of solemnity, but doubly handsome. Seriousness matched his presence, as if it were only to be expected that romantic heroes should brood, just as villains should sneer and heroines think clean.

Jason had dark eyes and classic features. His nose, square chin and cheekbones were as prominent as his tall brow was flat. The mouth was strong, the lower lip determined. Dark, long, shaggy hair formed a satisfying frame for the grave, handsome picture.

"Miss Harris," Jason said, his voice now with more command, "when you wake up you will find that you are cured. You will no longer have the habit of biting your fingernails. You will be happy about it. You will not worry. You will be greatly relieved. Should you ever get the urge again, you will smile at the foolishness of it, and be delighted that your nails are so lovely and long."

Jason talked on in this vein. To aid the girl, give her a manual substitute, he told her that she would buy a buffer and would use it whenever she recalled her delight in having long fingernails.

"When I rap the desk, Miss Harris, you will come awake." He gave the rap.

The girl opened her eyes, blinked, leaned forward from the chair back and looked at the turntable. "It's stopped," she said.

"Yes. It's all over. Treatment concluded."

She sat even straighter. "But what about hypnotising me?"

This was normal. A good half of subjects refused to believe they had been entranced. Jason said as much. The girl seemed unconvinced and paid the fee sulkily. As she was being ushered into the dark street she said, cheering up:

"But just in case you did it, I think I'll buy one of them buffer things."

Jason returned to the office, whose shabbiness was nearly hidden by new coats of paint. He stood and looked around. His eyes were crinkled with both amusement and dismay as he took in his surroundings and thought of Miss Harris' problem. They were a long way from the ideal.

Before the Vanetti Affair reached its unsatisfactory climax, Jason had been envisioning a bright future, one made possible by the fame and proceeds of his success. The money would come in the form of grants—from governments, schools, foundations, general charity. He would use it to create a laboratory-clinic and employ the finest minds in the field.

The work would be dedicated solely to producing empirical evidence in every facet of hypnotism. The answers to many riddles would be found. What exactly was the trance state? Whom did the subject believe the controlling voice to be? Was it possible to destroy free will?

The potentials of child-science hypnosis were enormous. It may be that a recidivist's criminal tendencies could be erased. It may be possible to cure all diseases of the mind, from neurosis to psychosis. It may, highest of all, be possible to cure via mass hypnosis the truly crippling diseases of mankind—bigotry, racism, intolerance, untruth.

That was the ideal. In its place, Jason was working not in the name of science but for himself, earning a living as the partner of a hypnotherapist, helping people give up cigarettes and minor obsessions, marking time.

If the Vanetti Affair had come out right, Jason began to muse. He stopped himself. He felt guilty enough already about Elsie.

After switching off lights, Jason locked the office and set off along the suburban shopping street toward the Underground station. He huddled his shoulders against the night's chill. As soon as he had cash to spare, he told himself, he would buy a topcoat. That's what he should have done instead of investing in these conformers, the jacket and pants.

At the Underground station, Jason bought a ticket and got on a train. Fifteen minutes later he came up to street level in Camden Town. The area was cheerfully grimy and cruel, like the chimneysweeps who used to light fires under their boy assistants to drive them up the flue. There had been few changes here since Dickens was a social reformer. The brash new store fronts looked as awkward as a halo on a pimp.

Soon Jason turned into Shank Place. Only half of its streetlamps were operating, which helped hide the decay, the decrepit cars and the obscene suggestions scrawled in chalk.

The dead-end street owned without enthusiasm a dozen houses. Each stood alone, but so close to the neighbours that it could only have been snobbery of perversity, a hundred years ago, which had kept the builder from creating solid rows.

The houses were identical—stucco finish, pillared portico up four steps, bay windows, low front wall to protect a rubbishy front yard six feet deep. Some properties had windows and doors blocked with corrugated iron to keep out squatters. The street was condemned.

Jason unlocked the door of number nine. He was met by a smell of damp. Ground floor and top floor were untenanted, and unfit to be otherwise. Bare boards covered the hallway and the broad flight of stairs.

To dispel the loneliness, Jason climbed noisily to his flat, the middle floor. The landing, bare, open to the staircase, served as access to the living room, bedroom, bathroom and kitchen, the last three bleak and typical of the street's terminal condition, the first as homey as used furniture and a man's hand could make it.

Jason switched on a transistor, set flame under the kettle, whistled, changed into jeans and a sweater—putting his business clothes carefully away and disliking the necessity for doing so.

Coffee made, he drank it while listening to the news on the radio. Police were still battling London's latest crime wave. Jason knew London rarely had waves of crime, only steady swells; the waves were combed by the media when all else was still and boring.

He went back to the kitchen to look at cans and plan supper. He told himself he wasn't lonely. Not a bit. And anyway, he would be seeing Elsie tomorrow night.

Jason became brisk in preparation of his meal.

About Elsie Vanetti, Jason had mixed emotions. On one side, he felt guilt for having held her an uncomfortable prisoner, and for the present possibility that what made him continue to see her might be an unconscious hope of, via her name and money, attaining his career ideal. On the other side, he was always happy when with Elsie, and thought he might be in love with her. It was only a thought on account of him never having experienced love; he didn't know the symptoms; and he felt that perhaps he was only excusing himself in this because of ulterior motive, which brought him round again to the ideal, and guilt.

Jason's anger on hearing of Hull Rainer's return to the Lancaster Gate flat, he had put down to dislike of the man, not jealousy. He was surprised himself at how abrupt he had been with Elsie when she had told him, and how cold to Rainer when they had met. Rainer had been the reverse, smiling and friendly.

Jason couldn't understand what Hull was doing there. For all the actor knew, Elsie could suddenly regain her memory, and his life would again be in danger. How could he sleep soundly? The man must be as stupid as he looked.

Jason knew there was no danger. He owned Elsie's memory and had no intentions of parting with it entire. When on occasion he gave her a pearl from his collection, it was always one from the beginning of the string, and then only reluctantly, surrendering because her need to know herself seemed so desperate.

After eating his supper, a frugal beans on toast, Jason went into the living room to dawdle away the evening. He read bits of a paperback, listened to the transistor, tried the crossword in yesterday's paper, thought about tomorrow night.

At eleven o'clock he yawned—gratefully. He got up to switch off the radio, stayed his hand to listen to the headlines of a newscast. What he heard made him gape.

Following a warning from the Bank of England of a new low in the economy, came: "Elsie Vanetti, the famous actress who disappeared ten weeks ago and was eventually found suffering from loss of memory, was taken from her London home this evening by an armed man. It is believed she has been kidnapped."

Jason went on gaping through the rest of the headlines and

details of the bank's warning, then sparked alert for the pertinent item, striding to the breakfront and bending over his transistor.

There was little to add. Miss Vanetti's husband had been assaulted, no one as yet had seen the actress and her abductor leave the building, Scotland Yard was investigating, roadblocks had been set up.

Jason switched off the radio and straightened slowly. He was incredulous. Elsie kidnapped—he thought. Fantastic. Nonsense.

Hurriedly he went downstairs. He left the house and ran all the way to the nearest telephone booth. Inside, panting, he clumsily fed the coin slot and dialled Elsie's number. A man answered. A stranger, not Rainer.

Jason said, "I've just heard on the radio—"

"Yes, sir," the man cut in briskly. "Do you have any information?"

"What? Oh, no. I'm checking to see if it's true."

"It's true, sir."

Jason insisted, "Elsie Vanetti has been kidnapped?"

"Exactly, sir. Now, may I ask you please not to call again unless it's urgent. We need the telephone. Goodnight." The line hissed dead.

Jason put down the receiver and went slowly outside. He still didn't believe it. He didn't want to believe it. He hated the thought that what he himself had done could have given someone the idea for a genuine kidnapping, that because of his selfish one-time hopes Elsie might . . .

He left it there, began to walk quickly. Every few steps he glanced behind at what little there was of approaching traffic. A taxi came along. It was engaged. Jason broke into a run. Two more engaged cabs passed before he found one that was vacant. He hailed it, got in, gasped, "Lancaster Gate."

On the quiet roads of night, they were there in ten minutes. Jason got out on Bayswater Road and paid off the cab. He stood staring up at the apartment building. The windows of Elsie's flat blazed light.

Jason crossed the road, circled the block, stopped at the corner. By the entrance to the building stood a constable, also several men who had the slouch of practiced waiters—journalists. At the kerb were two police cars. Across the street a group of people were staring.

Jason believed. He watched pointlessly and frustratedly for a time before turning away and setting off to walk home. It took him an hour to reach Shank Place, another three hours of pacing his flat to reach the point where physical weariness was strong enough to break through his preoccupation.

Fully dressed he lay on the bed and covered himself with a blanket. His mind continued its four-way seesawing among worry, shame, fear and anger. He felt useless. He knew now in full the enormity of his act ten weeks before. His body alternately tensed, slackened despondently, twitched with nerves. One name came to him time after time: that of Elsie's husband.

It was dawn when Jason fell asleep.

————◄◆►————

The room had walls of bare stone. The ceiling, low, had beams that sagged in the middle, like plays with padded second acts. The floor was hard-packed dirt.

The place measured about fifteen feet by twenty, Elsie reckoned. She also reckoned it was a cellar. Because of the crudity of finish, it could only be that or an outbuilding, and an outbuilding would have had windows. Here there were none. Ventilation seemed to come from a hole in a high corner; light was supplied by a naked bulb above.

Last night, being led in pitch darkness from the van, numb after a cold, uncomfortable ride, she had been aware only of entering a building, where, still dark, the man had moved with the sureness of familiarity. There had been three or four steps down, a stone floor, and then she had been pushed into this brightness ahead of a slammed door.

The room had obviously been furnished for the occasion. The bed was a simple cot with an iron frame, ex-army. Between it and the door stood a narrow table and one upright chair. Opposite, a heavy cable came through a wall crack to feed an electric fire, which, like the bulb above, was on constantly.

In a corner behind a screen (the prudery of which had made Elsie smile, momentarily forgetting the situation) was a portable lavatory of the chemical type, new and stamped with its brand name of Elsan. Also shielded there from view were basin and water jug, soap and towel. The screen was made of four sections of plywood, hinged.

Elsie had examined everything closely the night before, and again this morning. The arrangement was neat. Whoever her abductors were, they meant business, and had planned with care.

She was walking around the room, staying busy to keep from thinking. Fear, a new experience to her sixty-day-old mind, was like nausea being forced by fingers rammed down the throat.

Elsie looked at her watch. Nine o'clock. She continued circling, with stops to warm her hands at the electric fire. Her coat lay on the cot; she was saving it until she felt thoroughly chilled.

Still holding fear off, Elsie concentrated on reliving the journey in the small van—its colour was grey, she knew, and she also recalled that the number plate had been obscured with mud.

Although unable to see out, body windowless and blocked from the driver by a tin panel, she had been able to hear clearly enough. Traffic noise had gradually faded from dense to sporadic to nil. Toward the end she had heard the lowing of a cow. There had been no sound during the transfer from van to house, just as there had been silence since.

Elsie reckoned that unless the driver had played it smart, driving around for half an hour until stopping in some quiet suburb, and even imitating a cow, it was safe to assume she was in the country.

Not that it mattered, she thought. Except—yes—subterfuge

was better. It, the mask, all the precautions, they meant that later she would be unable to identify places and people, which meant she was not going to be harmed, which meant she had nothing to fear.

Elsie felt no better. And she caught her breath now and whirled as the door suddenly burst open.

The man came in. Except for his gloves, he wore the same outfit. In one of the hands supporting a tray of food, he held the gun.

The bottom part of the weird mask moved as the man spoke. "Get back against the wall, dearie."

Elsie went backwards, her eyes on the revolver. She was telling herself urgently she mustn't make any sudden, startling moves.

Watching her the while, the man slid the tray onto the table, reached his left hand to the door, locked it and slipped the key in his pocket.

"There we go," he said. "All nice and safe. Did my lady sleep well?"

"Not very," Elsie mumbled.

"Too bad. Never mind. Here's a good breakfast. I hope you're hungry."

Thinking there was no sense in being distant with the man, Elsie raised her voice to say, "Not very, thank you."

"Must eat, y'know. I fixed you a nice feed. Two boiled eggs, bread and butter, coffee. Nor did I forget the newspaper. Here, read all about it." He tossed the paper onto the bed.

Elsie took her eyes off the gun and went across. Sitting, she lifted the tabloid. Its headline yelled ELSIE VANETTI SNATCHED over a large picture of herself and a smaller one of Hull. A sub-banner said HUSBAND OF STAR PISTOL-WHIPPED BY MASKED MAN. Elsie read on, aware in the background of her mind that the stranger was muttering something about the electric fire.

Hull, Elsie was relieved to learn, had not even needed medical treatment. He had seen the abductor and had been able to give the police a description, which was being withheld for the present. A demand for ransom was expected soon. There seemed to have been no witnesses to the abduction. Anyone having seen unusual activity in the Lancaster Gate area was asked to contact the authorities.

Elsie was still reading—a recap of her first disappearance—when she became aware that the man was crouching over the fire with his back turned. She looked up. What she saw made her body jerk with fear.

The gun was on the table.

The man, perhaps in a moment of forgetfulness, or thinking she was too immersed in reading to notice, had put down the gun to tend to the fire. He was muttering that it should be hotter.

Elsie had fear because she knew she must take this chance; there might never be another. She must risk trying to get the gun in order to escape. If she failed, she could be beaten or killed.

It was an insane risk, but she knew she had to take it.

Quietly, she put down the paper. Quietly, she heeled off her shoes. Quietly; she began to rise from the bed—and froze when a spring whined.

The man seemed not to notice. He mumbled, "Should've brought a screwdriver."

Elsie stood erect, though not fully so. Her body was arched like a predator or a thief ready for the escape. Her heart thudded, her eyes tingled with staring.

The table was eight feet away. The tray of food lay in the middle. Beyond it was the revolver.

Elsie looked at it as she took one soft step forward. Of the weapon itself she had no fear, unlike most women. This she didn't question. Although she owned no memory of the coaching she had once received from a firearms expert for a movie role, the basics of the lessons remained. She could be at her ease with a gun without knowing why.

She took another step, this one longer. Her arms were out at the sides for balance. If the man glanced around now he would see her intention. But it was too late to go back.

While afraid, Elsie was also elating, *I am not a coward.*

She went another step forward. Fixedly she stared at the stranger, seeing the crown of his hat, the stocking leg tucked into his boilersuit neckline. The details were incredibly clear.

Three feet to go. She could have touched this end of the table by reaching. The man moved.

He shuffled his shoulders, changed from a crouch to a one-leg kneel. "Bloody thing," he grumbled. "Never was any good."

Elsie breathed again, and to her own ears the sudden intake of air sounded as loud as a gale. Her body was beginning to ache with its tension. She felt as though she could fall at any second.

So it's now or never, Elsie urged herself. Do it quickly.

Dispensing with silence and caution, she covered the remaining distance in a single stride. She grabbed for the gun.

The man twisted his head around.

Elsie's unsteady hand clattered against the tray. The cup of coffee slopped, the plates chinked. The gun skittered from her clawed fingers and slapped against the wall.

"Hey!" the man shouted. He shot to his feet and turned.

Elsie gave a noisy gasp like someone hit in the stomach. Her heart was jabbed with pain. Crouch more pronounced and face wild, she made another grab for the revolver.

The man was dashing towards her.

She got hold of the gun. She brought it into both hands. Fumblingly she turned it around so that she had it by the grip. She swung to face the man, who was now right beside her.

His arm came around in a mighty slap. It hit her hand. The gun jumped free of the shocked fingers. It went flying across the room.

Elsie and her enemy pushed at each other as they both moved forward in chase of the weapon. The next moment, incredibly and wonderfully, the man seemed to trip over his boots. With a snarled shout he fell on his face.

Elsie ran to the far wall. She picked up the gun and held it firm. She aimed it and said a breathless, "Get up."

The man was on his hands and knees. Looking at her, he said quietly, "Careful now."

"No, *you* be careful. Get up."

"That thing's loaded."

Elsie said, "Fine. Then you'd better watch yourself. Come on. Get up."

The man rose slowly, his hands held away from his body, palms up. He asked, sounding frightened, "You wouldn't shoot me, would you?"

"If I had to, yes. You would me."

"No, I wouldn't. Straight."

"Put your hands on top of your head."

He obeyed as he said quickly, "Don't kill me. Please. I didn't mean any harm. I wasn't going to hurt you. I'll let you go. I'll—"

"Be quiet!" Elsie snapped, not with toughness but because she felt like babbling herself and was afraid she might. "Move over against the wall."

"Believe me, lady," the stranger said as he stepped backwards. "I wasn't going to keep you. I'd just decided to call it off. I felt sorry for you cooped up in here. Please don't kill me." He stopped moving, his back to the wall.

Elsie ordered, "Bring one hand down slowly and get the key out of your pocket."

Instead of the expected obedience, the man made a weird noise at the back of his throat. It sounded like an animal in pain. He sagged against the wall.

Unnerved, Elsie gasped, "No tricks!"

The man continued to wail. His arms came down slowly and folded across his chest. He rocked his head from side to side like indecision.

"Stop it!" Elsie shouted, yet she knew somehow this was no act.

The stranger was bending forward over his arms, teetering gently. His legs were half bent. He made grunting sounds.

With that grotesque face, he looked like the fire victim she had first taken him to be, one newly staggered from the flames.

Elsie stared in growing horror. Next, the horror rushed to full force as she realised the truth. The man was laughing.

Feebly she asked, "What? What is it?"

Between wheezes, in a mocking tone of self-impersonation, the man said, "Don't shoot, lady, don't shoot."

"What?"

The man shook his head, laughing on.

Elsie knew. She lifted the gun close to her eyes. The weapon, she saw, was a toy. The split barrel was blocked, the plastic butt said Roy Rogers Special.

She closed her eyes briefly. She let the revolver drop to the floor as hope and tension died in her and her body sagged.

"Oh, Jesus," the man said, sighing his way to recovery. "Oh Christ. That was rich. You fell for it and no mistake."

Elsie said a dull, "You bastard." Her eyes filled with tears.

"Nothing wrong with a bit of a laugh, dearie."

"A toy. Just a toy."

"Well, now," the nam said, straightening, "I'm not such a fool as to leave a real gun lying around, nor to use one in the first place to grab someone."

Elsie stared. Her enemy added, "That's asking for big trouble in court."

Elsie tightened her lips. Anger was coming. That he had deliberately set a trick and played her along in fear and hope was bad enough; the fact of him getting her here by use of a toy was too much.

"You rotten bastard," she said. Clenched fists raised, she strode forward.

The man came to meet her. He grabbed her wrists. With no trace of humour in his voice he said, "Take it cool, dearie."

She wrenched to try to free herself. "Rotten bastard. Let me go." She longed to rake her fingernails over that strange semblance of a face.

Struggling, they moved across the room, Elsie in retreat.

The man said, "My shotgun in the other room's no toy. And it's loaded. You better calm down before I get annoyed."

Although her anger was seeping, under the approach of despair at the ease with which the man maneuvered her, Elsie was not ready to give in. She struggled until she felt the bed touch the backs of her legs.

She fell over. The man stayed with her. They lay one on top of the other on the bed, both breathing heavily. Their faces were close. Elsie turned hers away.

She said tersely, "Get off me."

"No hurry."

"Please. Let me up."

All he did was release her wrists, which brought his body closer to hers. His knee was between her legs. His hips began to insinuate gently.

Elsie hissed, "Get off me."

In a low, soothing tone, the man said, "You should be nice to me, y'know. We could spend some happy hours here together, you and me."

"Pig. Dirt. Bastard."

He slid up his right hand and covered her breast. She put a hand on his and tried to move it. It gave not a fraction.

She was ignoring the pressure of his hips and keeping her thighs clamped tight to his leg.

"Just fancy. Just imagine. Little old me lying on a bed with the beautiful and famous Elsie Vanetti."

Elsie wanted to spit in his face. She was afraid to. She asked, "Is this why you brought me here?"

"Don't be silly, love. The boys and me, we have big plans. But this is pretty good, eh? This is better than being all on your lonesome."

"Let me get up. Please."

"I will if you give us a kiss," he said. He went on cuddling and stroking her. Through the layers of clothing she felt nothing but the weight.

Attempting again to divert him, and with her face still turned away, Elsie asked, "How long will you keep me here?"

"Kiss me and I'll tell you."

"Go to hell."

"Listen, dearie," he said, his voice taking on a more businesslike tone. "I can tell you lots of little things. The boys don't need to know about it. All you have to do is co-operate. I'm a great one for the co-operation."

"Let me up and we'll talk."

"Nothing to talk about. You think this over. I can help you in lots of ways. And from you I only want a little co-operation. Understand?"

"No."

He took his hand off her breast and pushed himself up. "Yes, you do. Think about it." Moving toward the door, he called back, "See you later."

───────◆───────

Going down in the elevator, Hull Rainer arranged his features into a solemnity to match his dress, like a mortician putting down a comic book when the doorbell rings.

Hull was in a dark-blue suit, grey shirt, dark tie. As well as fitting for the circumstances, the outfit would also show up well on TV. Other touches were a piece of sticking plaster behind his ear and faint smudges of mascara under his eyes.

Hull was happy and excited. All was going according to plan. The police had left late last night and been back earlier this morning, but now had gone again. They hadn't been too much of a bore. Because of knowing about the abductor's gloves, there had been no messy search for fingerprints; because of the ransom demand being expected by mail, no bug had been put on the telephone.

Which, Hull thought, wouldn't stop them tapping it without letting him know. So he and Reece would stick to the plan of not using the phone. Anyway, it was getting enough use. Everyone from Elsie's mother to that bloody hypnotist had called for news.

But Hull was not suspected—and that was almost a disappointment. Chief Inspector Harold Wilkinson was again in charge of the case, as hoped, along with Detective-Sergeant Bart. There had not been, however, any of the open or veiled charges of involvement which had smeared the air that first time. Wilkinson had even acted sympathetic, and had apologised that because of the crime wave he wouldn't be able to give the case his undivided attention.

The elevator stopped, the doors hissed back. Hull stepped out into the lobby and walked to the entrance. He pushed outside and into his first press conference of Vanetti Affair II, produced and directed by Hull Rainer, written by Hull Rainer from his own original idea, and starring Hull Rainer.

There were reporters and photographers jostling for position with the grimness of ship passengers in line for the only lifeboat. Bumper to bumper at the kerb stood three trucks of rival TV networks, their cameras aimed, their umbilicals trailing to mike-holding interviewers.

Hull was surrounded. He talked, saying nothing novel or of value but saying it in grave style.

Yes, he was worried sick. He expected a ransom demand soon. He was praying Elsie would be returned to him unharmed; they were more in love than ever. Yes, he thought a gang was involved. No, it couldn't be a personal enemy. Yes, the police tracker dog had established that Elsie had been taken down to the garage. Yes, she had been wearing . . .

At one point, Hull contrived to look behind him, thus displaying for the cameras that poignant piece of sticking plaster behind his ear. He also got in the occasional wince with hand to brow.

Finally Hull said, "Gentlemen, that's all for now. There's an eleven o'clock Mass I want to attend." Get God in whenever possible, that was Hull's theory. "So if you'll excuse me."

With a wave-salute which would have looked better aimed at a multitude below a balcony, Hull turned and went back inside. Passing through a door he descended to the garage.

Beautiful, he thought. It had been beautiful. They'd lapped it up like cream spiked with scotch. The later papers would be even better than this morning's, just as the affair would grow from national to worldwide.

Whistling, he got in his MGB sports, yammered the motor to life and drove up the ramp.

Hull's idea for gaining international attention was to have Elsie appear to be not a kidnap victim, which was sordid, but a hostage, which had a hint of the noble. The ransom would be a person, not money. And the person would be of political consequence.

Although Hull had not made a final decision—enjoying the delay—he had his mind on a Russian spymaster who had been in an American prison for the past eight months, on a sentence of twenty years. The offered exchange would create a thumping international incident, and global headlines, at the centre of which would be a distraught Hull Rainer, begging everyone to get together for the sake of the woman he loved. The affair would go on and on: questions in the House of Commons, statements from the White House, enraged denials from the Kremlin.

In his lower stomach Hull felt a tingle of excitement, the unexpected bonus. This exact feeling he had experienced previously only with his girl friends. It came when he was unable to resist gaining a greater thrill, even though aware of the danger, which was possibly part of that thrill; and watching their faces carefully began to tell the girls in a calm voice that they were filth, tarts, tramps, gutter-fodder. It was much better than sex.

A blast on a car horn brought Hull aware he was driving too fast. Slowing, he told himself not to get carried away by the excitement, except when he was alone at home.

"You've got to watch yourself, Albert," he said.

After a five-minute drive, Hull stopped near a church. He got out of the car, locked it and walked away. On the first corner he halted to look back. He saw no signs of a tail, but knew a professional at the game would not be in evidence. Even so, he felt he had not been followed—especially after Wilkinson's lack of suspicion.

Hull thought he would still stick to the routine, of which this was a trial run—he was not expected at the farm this first day. Best to be safe. And if not the police, an enterprising reporter might take a notion to do some tailing.

Hull walked on. He came into a business district. One of the stores was a small Woolworth's. He went inside, entering the soapy smell and the useful crowding. Only one person looked at him with a frown of uncertain recognition as he walked to a rear doorway marked WASHROOMS.

Through there, at the end of a passage, a door led Hull to a yard lined with packing debris. As he crossed it he brought from an inside pocket a cap, folded flat. He opened it and put it on. From the other pocket he took a scarf, which, when he had wrapped it around his neck, hid his shirt and tie. The glasses with heavy black frames and plain glass were in his outside breast pocket. He took them out and put them on.

Emerging on an alley, Hull strode along to the right. He took off his piece of sticking plaster and put it away. The street he came out on was semibusy. He crossed it to a taxi rank, the first of whose waiting cabs he got in and said in a Scottish accent, "Drummond Road, please."

After glancing behind and seeing the all-clear, Hull sat back. He was enjoying himself, knowing he was clean helped. This was a part of the scheme he had been opposed to, the covert getting to the farm each afternoon. But David Reece had insisted.

If intercepted at this stage, Hull owned a plausible story to cover his bizarre actions and change of appearance. In this district (which is why it had been chosen during the planning) lived a woman of his own age, therefore above abuse, with whom he had been carrying on a casual relationship for many years, and whom he had been to see only three days ago for a rekindling.

She, Hull would sadly and reluctantly explain, was in love with him. He went to see her whenever he could, though naturally he didn't want word of this association to get out.

A similar situation pertained in Drummond Road, where

Hull paid off the cab. Being a lifelong philanderer had certainly had its uses.

As Hull strode along the street, heading for an Odeon cinema he could see farther on, he was reminded by his surroundings of the North London suburb in which he had grown up. The lower middle-class ambience had stifled him; his divorced mother's attitude to the male of the species had crippled him; his four younger sisters had derided him: he was the family dogsbody, workhorse, butt. It had been a great relief to escape into the lesser rigours of army life, to there hide on cherished occasion Private Green in battalion theatricals, and to bury him later with the enrollment of Hull Rainer in the Royal Academy of Dramatic Art.

Reaching the movie house, Hull turned into an alley at its side. Behind the building he came to a car park. The gateway was guarded from a glorified sentry box by an old man. He had red eyes and a drip on the end of his nose, like the *before* picture in ads for cold cures.

Recognising the newcomer from his two previous visits, the guardian came out to complain about the weather and his poor wage. Hull allowed the fraternisation, which normally he would have avoided, for he didn't want to make himself memorable by being abrupt. He spoke with an Australian accent and gave the man a medium-size tip.

Hull walked on to his car, the English Ford he had hired for a month and had paid to have parked here for the same period. He got in and drove off.

Two blocks away, on a quiet street, he stopped and got out. He looked back. He was sure now. No one had followed. He got in the car and drove on, stopping again by a telephone booth.

David Reece answered on the second ring. "Apple Acres. Hello."

"Hello, Dave," Hull said. "Larry here."

"Oh, sure. Hi there, Larry."

"How're the rabbits coming along?"

Reece said, "Great, just great. Not a problem in the world. How's tricks with you, Larry?"

"Couldn't be better."

"That's nice to hear. Very nice."

"Um—those rabbits," Hull said. "Are they going to be all right?"

"Of course."

"You're not bothering them, are you?"

"Of course not. I don't know what you mean."

Sensing annoyance in the other man, Hull turned it off with, "Don't want them to get too used to you. You know."

"Listen. I only go in there at feeding time."

"And carefully."

"Oh, sure. Wouldn't want to let one of 'em get out, now would I?"

"That's the spirit, Dave. Safety first."

"Rely on me, Larry. I know what I'm doing."

"Right, then," Hull said crisply. "I'll pop over and see you tomorrow as arranged."

"Yes," Reece said, "you will. So long for now."

After putting down the receiver, Hull slid his fingers free rather than lifting them off. This would smear the prints. It was as unnecessary as had been the cryptic nature of the conversation, but he enjoyed it. He also enjoyed the casual look around as he got back in the car. He saw the scene as a long-shot first, then fast cut to a medium-close, POV the steering wheel. Real arty.

For thirty minutes Hull drove aimlessly around quiet streets. He entertained the idea of calling on the woman who lived in this area, deciding against it because (A) he wasn't in the mood, and (B) she might find it odd, him visiting so soon after the last call.

He returned the Ford to its parking slot, nodded at the guardian on his way out, and walked to the nearest Underground station. Unlike the journey here, he could vary the return.

He got on a train. Making a random choice, he alighted at

the second station. He had the tunnelled staircase to himself while taking off and putting away his disguise. He returned the sticking plaster to its place behind his ear.

Out of the station he went into a pub. The room was crowded with noontime drinkers. As Hull moved to the bar, the clamour of talk began to lessen. It had become a buzz by the time he had quietly ordered a gin and tonic. Those who hadn't noticed him were being told by those who had. The barmaid stood nearby with her mouth slightly open. There was a rustle of newsprint as the ignorant were shown the front-page pictures, or the knowledgeable checked for verification.

Hull was the focal point of every eye. He stood there with a worried expression and let himself be looked at. The moisture which came to dim his vision helped the image but was gratuitous, genuine. He felt emotional.

It's all happening: his thought soared. I'm back there again. This is what it's all about. I'm happy, so happy.

---

Jason was walking toward Shank Place, slapping the rolled newspapers against his leg. He was oblivious to the midday bustle around him. His features were set in an exaggeration of their usual solemnity, and a muscle in his jaw twitched like a pulse.

Because of Jason's lateness in getting to sleep, he had dozed on until noon. Awakening to find himself fully dressed, his first thought had been how odd it was, for this was where Elsie had slept in her clothes. Which caused him to recall what had happened.

He had checked his watch, leapt up, switched on the radio, gone into the bathroom to throw water on his face, come back to glare at the transistor as if it were to blame for not producing an immediate newscast.

Too impatient and fretful to wait, Jason had left the house and hurried to the nearest newsvendor's. He bought papers, devoured them with an exile's hunger in the street and while in a café mindlessly consuming coffee and donuts.

Jason gave his thigh a slap to match every thought in the chain he was forging, beginning with what he knew and the police did not.

Hull Rainer was well aware that he was in danger by going back to the Lancaster Gate flat. *Slap*. He could easily afford a hotel. *Slap*. He must have returned for a purpose. *Slap*. It was odd that he'd gone back just now. *Slap*. The abductor had been seen by no one—except Hull Rainer. *Slap*. That other man might not exist. *Slap*. Hull Rainer had no love for his wife, had cheated on her for years. *Slap*. He would no doubt feel better if she were permanently out of the way.

Jason didn't slap on that one. He didn't like it. But it seemed to fit, to follow. If, as he suspected, the actor was behind this, it could hardly be for money. There was no other possible motive.

But, Jason thought—and slapped his leg—Rainer could well be heavily in debt. His women, for one thing. Then, there could be gambling, money lost in backing plays, blackmail because of his sex life.

Jason felt better.

He noticed he had turned into Shank Place. Next, he saw that a car stood before number nine. Third, he knew somehow that although the car bore no insignia it belonged to the police.

Drawing closer, he saw he was right. He recognised the driver as Detective-Sergeant Bart, and the passenger as Chief Inspector Wilkinson. The two men were watching his approach.

Jason's stride became eager. Last time, he thought, the police had been enemies. Now they were allies.

Wilkinson got out of the car as Jason came abreast. The inspector looked to be in his mid-fifties. He had grey hair as dense as a scrubbing brush. His ruddy face was flat and vaguely Oriental. Suitably, it was impressive. His fawn raincoat also struck the right note.

Jason impulsively stuck out his hand. "Hello, Inspector. Any news?" He knew from the papers that Wilkinson was in charge of investigating Elsie's abduction.

Therefore he was surprised when, after giving a limp handshake, the senior detective asked, "News of what?"

"Elsie. Miss Vanetti."

"That's funny," Chief Inspector Harold Wilkinson said. "I was going to ask you that very same question."

Jason's friendliness chilled. He said shortly, "I'm not with you."

Detective-Sergeant Bart asked, "Been busy this morning, Mr. Galt?" He had one foot on the car's bumper. A tall, thin man, younger than Jason, he was bald and mournful-faced and had canopied eyes.

"Busy sleeping."

Wilkinson: "We came here earlier and knocked for five minutes. You must be a very sound sleeper, sir."

The last word pronounced like an insult. Jason said, "I am."

"Next we found out where you operate, and went there. Your partner, who thinks he looks like Svengali, said you were expected but hadn't showed up. We came back to wait."

"Terribly sorry you've been inconvenienced," Jason said heavily. "I slept late and then went out for the papers and breakfast."

Bart: "Is Jason Galt your real name, by the way? Sounds a bit phony. Is it a stage name?"

"Quite real."

"Okay. And what's the date and place of your birth, please?"

Jason frowned. "Why?"

Inspector Wilkinson said, "Scotland Yard files can tell us from that if you've got a record."

Jason snapped out the wanted details and added, "I have no record. I only have a burning desire to know what the hell you're after."

"We," Wilkinson said, "are investigating the abduction of Elsie Vanetti."

"I know."

"And we think you might be able to help us with our enquiries, as the phrase goes."

Jason said, "You think, in fact, that I did it myself."

"Someone did. You're as good a suspect as any. And if you have nice clean hands, I'm sure you'll want to do all you can to help."

Jason shrugged. He had forgotten about allies. He said, "I hate to see you wasting your time here. You should be talking to Hull Rainer."

Inspector Wilkinson brought out a pipe and looked into its bowl. "Mr. Rainer would hardly kidnap his own wife, in my view."

"Someone did."

The detective's return was, "You've been seeing a lot of Miss Vanetti. You might be able to help. Perhaps we could go inside?"

Jason turned away, went up the steps and opened the door. He stood aside. Wilkinson and Bart went in. The latter, in a voice of casual interest, said, "I like these old places." Hands clasped browserlike behind, he walked down the hall.

Jason closed the door. "Has there been a ransom demand yet?"

"If it's coming by mail," Wilkinson said, "it wouldn't arrive much before this evening, would it?"

"I suppose not."

Bart thudded into view from a back room. Before entering another he said, "Good and spacious."

Jason went to the stairs. "This way." He led Inspector Wilkinson up to the landing. "This is my flat. I live alone."

"Bachelor, Mr. Galt?"

"That's right."

"A neighbour tells us she thought you were married. There was a girl living here up till about three months ago."

"A friend."

"Care to tell me her name?"

"No, thank you. She's none of your business."

Detective-Sergeant Bart plodded up to join them. He said, "Yes, good big empty rooms."

"This way," Jason said again. He took the policemen into the front room. After tossing his papers onto the breakfront, he leaned back on it and folded his arms.

Inspector Wilkinson sat on the couch. He brought out a tobacco pouch and began to fill his pipe, asking, "Mind if Mr. Bart has a poke about?"

"I suppose not. But I could be awkward and ask for a search warrant."

"Do that, sir," Wilkinson said. He glanced to where his assistant was standing by the door. "Show him."

Bart came forward pulling a piece of paper from his pocket. He handed it to Jason, who looked at it more from curiosity than for confirmation. Disappointingly, a search warrant was a mere half page of typing illegibly signed by a magistrate.

He gave it back. "Why did you ask, if you already had this?"

Wilkinson tamped busily. "Wanted to see if you'd say no."

As Bart left the room, Jason told him there was some small change on the kitchen table. "Don't touch it. I know exactly how much there is."

Wilkinson made a grunting sound. It might have been a chuckle. He put his pouch away and almost showed expression—satisfaction—in gazing at his readied pipe.

Wanting to know without asking pointedly, Jason said, "I thought Hull Rainer was out of the country, making a film."

"No, he's here. Obviously."

"Maybe he just made a quick trip abroad."

"Possibly," Wilkinson said without interest, getting out a box of matches, which, predictably, he rattled. "He did mention having been away from home for a couple of days."

That, Jason thought, the true length of Rainer's absence from the flat, was something else he knew and the police did not, and formed another link in the chain. Turning, he picked up the rolled newspapers, slapped his leg, threw the papers down, turned back.

Wilkinson said, "You seem nervous, Mr. Galt."

"I am. A friend's in danger, and the top investigating officer is wasting his time."

The policeman did a seesaw movement with his shoulders. He struck a match, poised it over his pipe and asked an automatic, "May I smoke?"

"No," Jason said, "you may not."

Still impassive, Wilkinson blew out the match. He put the box away but kept his pipe, cuddling it in both hands.

"You're absolutely stunned, of course," he said, "that we should suspect you, and you're bursting to know why."

Jason listened to thumps from the landing, which signalled Bart's removal of the partition blocking the upper staircase. Next came the sound of ascending footsteps.

Jason asked, "What?"

Wilkinson made a mumble. It could have been annoyance. He said, "You appear on the scene two months ago and offer to restore the memory of Elsie Vanetti. You are going to charge an extremely nominal sum for said service, amazing in respect of your poverty. Your kindness is staggering. You certainly don't want any of the Vanetti money, do you?"

"I did not," Jason said, disliking the wrong tense.

Wilkinson, looking at his pipe, continued, "The hypnotism trick doesn't come off, which is too bad, especially with reporters—they're all ready to whoop it up. But you are not dismayed. It's sheer kindness again that makes you keep going back to the Vanetti flat. That the lady is rich and famous doesn't deter you, does it?"

"It did not."

"Never mind the hundreds of impoverished unknowns who need your help, you are going to go on helping Miss Vanetti, poor girl."

"Make up your mind," Jason said. "Am I a trickster or can I really help people?"

Wilkinson ignored him. He went on, "You're getting nowhere, so you decide to snatch the lady. You disguise yourself and pull the job and whisk the victim into hiding. You're all set."

"Fine," Jason said. "Now tell me why I did it."

The inspector looked up. "Money. A straight swap of victim for cash. Or, more devious, financial gain of a long-term nature: Miss Vanetti's gratitude, the spoils of fame."

Jason said, with honesty, "I'm not following you on that last bit."

"While you have the lady completely to yourself, no interruptions from husband and friends, you put her into a trance and give her back her memory. A memory. You tell her everything you know about Elsie Vanetti, which can be got from biographies. You slowly and carefully give her, in fact, a false past, and say she's cured."

This was so dangerously like the original truth, though in reverse, that Jason was startled. He felt for the policeman what he had denied him until now—admiration.

"Clever, Inspector," he said. "A lovely idea. But would I have to go to the trouble—and danger—of kidnapping the lady to give her an imitation memory? I could do it a bit at a time, whenever we met."

"That wouldn't have snap. Gradual recovery would be thought natural. You wouldn't get the thanks, the profit. Elsie has to spring to the fore all cured."

"After I'd rescued her, sword in hand, from the villainous kidnappers? They escape, of course, and are never seen again."

Wilkinson got up and put his pipe away. He said, "Most likely you'd say the kidnapping angle was not to be taken for real. You spirited the lady away from home for her own good. She, thinking herself cured, wouldn't charge you." He nodded. "But *we* would."

"It's full of holes, Inspector."

Detective-Sergeant Bart appeared in the doorway. "Empty," he said.

Wilkinson showed nothing. He didn't even make acknowledgement. Still looking at Jason, he said, "Or it's the other thing. An exchange for immediate cash."

Jason made the gesture of glancing at his watch. "If I've helped your enquiries enough for the time being," he said, "I'll go to work."

Inspector Wilkinson turned away. He threw back a terse, "Don't leave town."

Five minutes later, Jason, having heard the car drive off, put on his windcheater and zipped it up as he went briskly down the stairs. Outside he set off for the Underground. A taxi would have suited his urgency better, but he was getting short of money and thought he might need what he had for a greater emergency.

Striding, Jason mused on Wilkinson's suspicions. They meant little. The police had a standard gambit of accusing every suspect in the hopes of a quick confession, and it worked surprisingly often. The attitude now might rule out, however, a thorough investigation of Hull Rainer.

Jason was almost convinced of Rainer's complicity. The actor had not told the police of being separated from his wife. They were not liable to find out from anyone else, because Elsie and Hull had agreed to keep it quiet for the present, and Jason's information would be ignored as a red herring.

It's up to me, Jason thought. If rat Rainer's the one.

In the station he bought a ticket from a machine and hurried down to the platforms. A train was racketing in. He got aboard and, despite ranks of vacant seating, stood by the doors. Five fast stations later he got out at Tottenham Court Road and went to the Central Line platform. Here he was less lucky. Long minutes passed before a train arrived.

Racing nerves caused Jason to truncate the journey with one station yet to go. He got out at Marble Arch. It felt better to be walking, to be in control of propulsion.

A score of idlers stood across from the apartment house. They stared morbidly at the building and looked as if they'd be disappointed with anything less than a bloody corpse.

By the entrance lounged a solitary youth. Knowing something of the workings of the press, Jason surmised that the lad, a Fleet Street yearner, had been paid to wait here in case of developments, news of which he would then take to the reporters, waiting in comfort at the nearest pub.

Head lowered to signal disinterest, Jason entered the garage mouth and went down the ramp into gloom. He saw at once that the MGB wasn't present. But he wasn't relying on that fact.

Swiftly he climbed the service stairs. He had half expected the apartment to be guarded by a constable, but the corridor was deserted. He went to the door and rang the bell.

There was no answer. He knocked, waited a full minute, rang the bell again. There was no sound from inside.

Why isn't the frantic husband waiting at home for word from the kidnappers?—Jason mused in sarcasm as he went back down to the garage.

He moved to a position beside the ramp. By standing on a car's bumper he could see obliquely to the front of the building. Alternating standing there with pacing, he passed half an hour. Two cars came in and one went out—Jason hiding the while.

The third car to come in was the MGB. Crouching, Jason circled the parked vehicles while the convertible was being steered into its marked slot. He was standing waiting when Hull Rainer got out.

The actor turned, started back, gasped, "Jesus."

Jason said, "Hello."

Not accustomed yet to the change of light, Hull Rainer peered with slitted eyes. "Oh," he said. "It's you." He smelt faintly of gin. "Hello."

"Sorry I gave you a fright."

"It's okay."

"Didn't think you were nervous," Jason said, stealing one from Wilkinson.

Rainer ruffled himself, stretched up his neck. "What d'you want here anyway?"

"News of Elsie."

"There's no news, Galt. When there is, you'll read it in the papers." This was far from his Uriah Heep mien when he had returned to the flat a few days ago. He made to move past.

Jason blocked his way. He said, "The police came to see me this morning." He thought he could sense a sudden wariness in the other man, though Rainer's voice seemed casual when he asked, "What for?"

"They think I might have kidnapped Elsie."

Hull Rainer shrugged. "They'll be checking everybody, I imagine."

"You don't seem curious about what the police think. Maybe you know there's nothing in it."

"Eh?"

"Maybe you know where she is."

The actor looked startled again. "What does *that* mean?"

"Only kidding," Jason said, forcing a grin. "Actually, I came to tell you that Wilkinson was asking about you and Elsie. He wanted to know how you were getting along together."

Carefully: "Oh? Is that right? So what did you say?"

"That you got along famously, were always together."

There was a pause. The two men looked at each other. Jason said, "The second reason I came, I was wondering if you could loan me a few quid. I'd like to get out in the country for a few days, but I'm broke just now."

There was eagerness in Rainer's actions as he reached in his pocket, saying, "Glad to help you out, Galt. I know the feeling. Could do with a break myself. Here, twenty-one, two, three. Twenty-three pounds. That do?"

Guilty, Jason thought as he took the money. Whether payment was for past silence or future absence—guilty.

He wanted to grab the man by his slim, smooth neck and squeeze him until the truth squirted out like toothpaste. Instead, he shoved the money-holding fist in his pocket and clenched the other.

"Thanks," he said. "I'll pay you back as soon as I can."

"No hurry, Galt. Take your time. I've been short as well, in my day. I know how it is."

That Uriah Heep mien was back again, and so out of character. Jason's urge to try physical assault returned to full strength. It was like an itch that would drive him mad if he didn't scratch. But reason told him this affair was too big for Rainer to be made to talk out of fear or pain, and there was still the faint chance he might not be the one responsible.

"Well," the actor began, making those little motions and weaves which preface leaving. At which point Jason saw the perfect method. He couldn't stop himself from smiling. He also felt astonishment—at the fact that this way hadn't occurred to him sooner.

Rainer asked, "Mm? What's the joke?"

"Curious, funny," Jason said, "not humorous." He turned, his eyes rapidly searching for a suitable claimer of attention. It would not be easy. Everything in the garage was gloomy and dull.

Hull Rainer asked, "What is it?"

Jason said, "The police. There's a way they could've seen Elsie and the kidnapper leave."

Sharply: "Oh?"

He found what he could use. It was far from the ideal, but would have to do. The rest was up to him, and Hull Rainer's suggestibility.

Moving to stand beside the other man he clasped his shoulder and with the other hand pointed toward the gaping exit, the one patch of brightness. "See there, through the doorway, that car."

"Which car?"

"Blue one. Its back window catches the light. See that?"

Hull Rainer said, "Yes, I see it but what—"

"Listen. Listen carefully. This could be important. This might be a way to catch these people. That window could be the answer."

Jason glanced aside at Rainer's face, saw the eyes intent on the focal point, and said in a slow, deep voice, "Imagine someone sitting there behind that window. He can see out, but he can't be seen because of the shine on the glass. Perhaps he's tired. There's a lot on his mind, many worries, and he's feeling very tired. He's so tired that he doesn't know if he can stay awake. He doesn't really care. He's so tired. As tired as could be. He hasn't felt this tired for years."

Jason glanced aside again. Hull Rainer's eyes were fixed and dull, his features slack. Repetition was doing its work. Softly and soothingly, Jason went on:

"He's about to sleep, that man. Sleep. He wants to sleep. He wants to close his eyes and sleep. Sleep is good, sleep is peace, sleep is a blessing, sleep is the end of pain. He is sleepy."

Hull Rainer sipped in a long, chest-lifting breath and then released it in a sigh which had a light, petted moan.

"You can understand how he feels," Jason said crooningly. "You are sleepy as well. You have the same desire for sleep. You want a long and deep—"

With a roar, a car burst into the garage.

Hull Rainer jerked as if jabbed with a pin. Jason clamped his tongue to the roof of his mouth to keep from cursing. The car zoomed to a corner and stopped with a screech.

Hull looked all around before turning a bewildered stare on Jason. "What was that?" he asked. "What were you saying?"

"I'll get back to it in a minute. Let those people leave first."

A knowing look came into the actor's face. "No," he said, his voice quick and unsteady. "Never mind. It doesn't matter." He sidled past Jason and began to back off. "Forget it."

"Listen. Wait just one minute."

"No. I have to go. Forget it. You take that holiday, Galt. And you better stay away from here in future. I'm busy and the police don't want people around."

Turning abruptly, he strode off toward the service stairs. Jason watched him go from sight and then swung his fists in a brief surrender to fury and disgust. He knew he would never get another chance.

A young couple, laughing, alighted from the newly arrived

car and followed Rainer. Jason was glad he wasn't close enough to give them a kick.

He left the garage and headed in the direction of home. On the way were several nontourist districts, beginning with Paddington, where it would be possible to rent a car.

That Hull Rainer was involved in the kidnapping, was indeed the sole kidnapper, Jason had become sure, with only a shimmer of a reservation. Elsie was unlikely to be on the premises: she was being kept somewhere else: Hull would have to check on her regularly: he could be followed.

The actor, Jason thought, was going to regret that loan.

In Paddington Jason went into the railway station. There were two car-rental agencies. He chose the one with the smaller advertising budget. It was no help. The cost cowed his pocket. He complained, "That's a hell of a lot for a car."

"There's also a mileage charge," the man said. He was slickly dressed and had a supercilious expression like a show dog. He added, "Perhaps you would be better off with a motorbike, sir."

Although the man didn't mean it, was being facetious, Jason took to the idea at once. A car could lose another car in traffic, but not so easily a motorcycle.

"Thanks," he said.

Two hours later, after hard bargaining, paper signing and a practice drive, Jason was in possession of a black and chrome Norton. In a district near home, he drew the machine into the kerb and stopped.

He found an accessory shop, where he bought a white crash helmet, a pair of goggles, and a cheap plastic raincoat which came folded in a packet the size of a softcover book.

Outside again, he noticed an appliance store. In the window television sets were playing, silent behind the glass. He checked his watch. It was fifteen minutes to news time.

He went on, found a telephone kiosk, went in and dialled the Rainer-Vanetti number. The actor answered. He sounded bored.

Making his voice two octaves higher, Jason said, "Good afternoon, sir. I'm Andrew Wilson of *Time* magazine. We're considering doing a rush lead story on your wife's abduction."

No longer sounding bored, Hull Rainer said, "Oh, really?" As Jason had guessed, the man was unable to resist the call of free international publicity.

"It'll be more human interest than a warts-and-all of the investigation, so I understand. I'm a photographer, you see. I shan't be doing any writing so I'll have no questions. I'd just like fifteen minutes of your time."

"Yes, I see."

"Mainly I want a picture of you in your home, to go on the cover with one of Miss Vanetti."

"Ah, yes, Mr. Wilson," the actor said. "I think I can spare you fifteen minutes."

"Fine, sir. Will you be home all this evening?"

"Yes, I shan't be going out anywhere."

"Or I could make it tomorrow before twelve noon."

"That would be all right as well."

"Oh, sorry," Jason said. "Checking my worksheet here. I see I'm on another job in the morning."

"Then make it tonight."

"I'll try, but I want at least one alternative. We always work that way. How about tomorrow afternoon at three?"

Rainer said, "No can do, Mr. Wilson. I'm—I'm having people here. The police. Four would be okay, though."

"Good," Jason said, and decided not to risk trying to get closer than the established—before three and after twelve. Following another minute of flattery and sympathy, he disconnected.

He went back to the appliance store.

With two old men and a girl holding a child, Jason watched a program end and the news telecast begin; watched the commentator mouthing unheard words, one of which he lip-read as Vanetti, the rest of which he wasn't interested in because he knew there could be no new developments; watched Hull Rainer talking outside the apartment house and turning to show his best profile; and watched with an ache a movie clip of Elsie. Dressed in a long white gown, looking like everyone's dream of an angel, she slowly and gracefully descended a staircase.

---

Hair in ungainly hanks, clothes rumpled, a smudge of dirt on one cheek, Elsie sat on her heels in front of the electric fire. She was as low in spirit as her position, as cold inside as her feet, as dreary of feature as her prison.

Elsie had been here twenty-four hours. It felt like a week. She had stopped thinking of escape, which seemed a foolish improbability, and was dreaming of even greater unlikelihoods: a hot bath, a comb, cups of scalding tea, snacks, a book.

The last especially. Empty time is a hardship for someone who has no recall; and that, the lack of remembered experience, limits imagination to the mundane. Elsie had escaped the walls only in thoughts of Jason Galt.

At midday, when the man had brought in a piece of meat pie and a mug of lukewarm coffee, she had asked him if he could give her something to read.

"You got the paper, dearie."

"I've finished it," Elsie said. "Haven't you any books?"

"A nice crime story, eh? Maybe about a beautiful girl that gets kidnapped."

She resisted telling him he had an ugly sense of humour. "Anything would do. Anything at all."

"Tell you what," he said, rubbing his stocking-covered chin, "I'll find you a book if you'll give me a little kiss."

Elsie had turned away, ignoring the rest of his suggestive talk, and statements that all he wanted was a bit of co-operation.

She got up stiffly and went over to the bed. She lifted the newspaper. Its every word was familiar. She knew its post office registration number, through familiarity was contemptuous of the photographs, had scratched in the solvable clues of the crossword, knew the price of every item in Harrod's autumn sale.

Pacing, Elsie tried again to fill the blank spaces in the cross-word puzzle. Knowledge was the problem: Elsie found that while on the one hand she possessed abstruse facts, such as Sicily's Etna being 10,868 feet high, she was unable to put names to the most commonplace objects.

There came a metallic rattling. Elsie recognised the sound. It was the lock being keyed. Tossing the paper aside, she went to stand opposite the door.

It opened and the man came in. He was carrying the tray. For the first time, Elsie noticed that another door lay immediately behind the first, and that it was of new, heavy planking. Obviously it had been fitted for this occasion, a sound-proofing: shouts for help would go unheard, she would be unable to pick up identifying noises.

Elsie's spirits ebbed still further. The planning and foresight made an escape even more unlikely.

The man locked the door, pocketed the key, put down the tray. Elsie rallied at the sight of steaming soup, hunks of bread and a glass of milk.

When the man moved away, she went and sat down. Setting aside the evening newspaper, she began to eat.

"Good drop o' soup that," the man said. He sat far back on the bed and leaned his shoulders on the wall. "I'll be hurt if you leave any. Made it meself, out of a can. Like it?"

Between gulps, Elsie said, "Yes," and, "Thanks."

"There's the paper, too. Haven't really read it meself yet. That's good of me, I reckon, don't you? Hope you appreciate all these little favours. Not everyone'd do it for you. Kind, that's what I am."

Elsie had not seen her captor so at ease and gregarious before. This caused her to wonder if the affair were nearly over, settled. Swallowing a mouthful of soup, she asked:

"Are you going to let me go soon?"

"Sure. In ten minutes."

She twisted to face him fully. "What?"

The stocking mask wrinkled over his mouth. He said, "I'm going to let you go in the corner and wash your hands."

Elsie sighed, turned back and went on eating. She wiped up the last of the soup with bread, drank the milk. Still hungry, but eased, she sat back and hissed a belch into her fist.

"Manners," the man said. "I'm all for it." He got off the bed and came to stand behind her. Elsie made to rise from the chair. The man put his hands on her shoulders and held her down. She slanted her head forward, away from his cushiony stomach.

Voice low, the man said, "Yes, I'm all for a beautiful little lady doing the right things."

Elsie picked up the newspaper. She unfolded it and looked at the front page. The headline related to an economic crisis. The secondary banner told her she was still missing. There was a photograph of Hull outside the apartment building. Seeing home, Elsie experienced a pang.

Indifferently, she realised the man was running a hand up and down her upper arm. The lack of concern made her question if her resolve to hold him off was weakening.

Shaking the hand off with a push more annoyed than offended, Elsie said, "Let me read, please."

Grunting, he confined himself to a gentle kneading of her shoulders.

Elsie read down the columns of type. It was all she already knew—until an item near the bottom. Voicing a thought, she said, "That seems an awful lot of money."

"What does?"

"A Hollywood studio has announced it's just paid me my first percentage."

The man sounded alert. "Percentage of what?"

"Profit. My cut on the last movie. It's been doing boom business in the last couple of months, Hull told me."

"How much is your cut?"

Carelessly, Elsie said, "Over half a million dollars."

First the man said a shocked-sounding "What?" Next he grabbed the newspaper away from her. Elsie got up and moved over to the wall. She watched the man reading avidly.

He said, ". . . a check sent to Miss Vanetti's London agent for five hundred and forty thousand dollars." He lowered the paper. "Suffering Christ."

"There'll be taxes and agent's fees to come off that," Elsie said, and wondered how she knew.

"Still a bloody fortune."

"I suppose it is a lot."

"Listen," the man said. "I thought all actors were poor. The one's I've ever known were always broke."

So, Elsie thought, you have some connexion with the theatre. She said, "Not many save anything, it seems."

He threw the newspaper on the table as if it had offended him. "A fortune. A bloody fortune."

Because he appeared so concerned, therefore not interested in her, Elsie began to talk about earnings in the acting profession. She gave names she had recently acquired and matched them with invented sums of money. The man watched her, nodding.

He said, "Millionaires."

"Only a handful. The rest could make more money by waiting on tables." It was a phrase Jason had used.

Where was Jason now?—Elsie mused. Was he worrying? Was he trying to find her? Or was he not overly concerned, she being to him merely an interesting, challenging case study?

Becoming aware that the man had spoken, she said, "I'm sorry."

"I asked what happens to this Hollywood money."

"Well, from what I understand, it goes into my account. I have two. One's a joint checking account I share with my—my husband." She always had trouble getting that out. "The other's regular."

The man nodded. He lifted the tray and, surprisingly, said, "See you tomorrow." It was surprising because he usually lingered to talk.

Relieved that there were going to be no passes made, verbal

or otherwise, still Elsie risked breaking the man's preoccupation by asking, "How about something to read?"

"You got two newspapers," he said curtly. "That's enough
for anybody."

---

"God damn it to hell," Hull growled. He turned over,
thumped the pillow viciously, flopped down again. The bed
felt like a rock. Hull pitied himself for his inability to sleep.
He thought, If only people knew what I went through.

It was after midnight. Every time Hull had veered close to
a doze, he had been visited by one of the scheme's unattrac-
tive or potentially dangerous aspects.

Leading the former was his recollection of David Reece,
agreement to participate concluded, licking his lips and saying, "Me and Elsie Vanetti here alone together. Well, well,
well."

As for danger, recurring was Hull's impression that Jason
Galt had tried to hypnotise him in the basement garage. He
sweated in crotch and armpit at the scene his imagination produced: himself chanting out zombi-like to Galt all the details
of the plot.

The scene began to come again now. Hull chased it by sitting up and clicking on the bedside light. It hadn't happened,
he assured himself, and it wasn't going to. The hypnotist
would be avoided—whether or not he went away. And the
risk of him telling the police about the Rainer-Vanetti separation, which he'd hinted at, that could be resolved.

Hull thought he could mention it himself, to Wilkinson. He
could say he had left Elsie for her own good, to see if she
would get her memory back if left alone. Something like that.
It was going to be great. No bad things were happening. And
*Time* magazine, baby. The cover, yet. Think about that.

Hull did. It made him more wakeful than ever. He got out
of bed and went in search of sleeping pills. The bathroom
medicine chest had nothing fiercer than aspirin. Hull went
into the master bedroom.

In a drawer of the vanity table he found some old tranquilizers. He chewed and swallowed two while examining himself in the mirror. When he noticed lines beside his mouth, he ignored them by pretending interest in the red smears on the glass where he had wiped off the lipstick message—after the police had photographed it an exorbitant number of times.

Hull turned and looked at the bed. He wondered about David Reece again. Was he bothering Elsie? Was he forcing her at gunpoint to submit?

Hull scowled. Though he had no love left for his wife, even the reverse—the bitch was a homicidal maniac—he still had proprietary feelings toward Elsie; though he didn't want her himself, he had no wish for her to be owned by anyone else, even briefly. There was also his loathing of violence.

Trouble was, he didn't know enough about Reece's personality. Hull groaned at the realisation that he had found something else to worry about in this nocturnal neuroticking.

Hull Rainer had met David Reece some five years before, when Hull had had a small part in a West End play. Management's policy was to allow the actors tickets at a cut rate for use of their friends, with an occasional complimentary pair. Hull sold all his to a scalper at the normal rate.

Unlike the other unofficial ticket sellers who hung around the theatre before curtain-up, buttonholing passers-by and soliciting the queues, David Reece wore no flash clothes or air of borderline criminality.

In his cheap, tidy suit he looked like a labourer up West for a night out. He also had a more subtle approach. His attitude was apologetic rather than brash. Often he would make a sale after another spiv had caused a would-be customer to sheer off warily.

Hull bought all the tickets he was allowed, plus giving a tithe on those obtained by his fellow actors, plus doing the same with colleagues in other theatres. Soon he was making more money than that earned by his role.

He did business with David Reece in a Soho pub. Often,

transaction done, Hull would stay on and talk over a glass of beer.

Reece, some half-dozen years older than Hull, was of medium height and build. He had a coarse, simian face. Recessed deeply under tangly black eyebrows, his eyes were sharp, alert, constantly darting like an auctioneer's. His hair had the consistency of wire wool and he always looked to be in need of a shave. Not helping were the blob nose, broken teeth, lips of disproportionate thickness.

One day in the pub, Hull and David Reece were talking about the origin of the slang word *spiv*, one who lives by his wits in society's lower levels. The scalper said he thought it came from "spiff," a flashy person. Hull's offer was that he believed it came from the initial letters of the police's Suspected Person or Itinerant Vagrant.

"I did hear too," Reece said, "as it was VIPs backwards. The reverse, see. Very *un*important person."

"You're knocking yourself, Dave."

Smiling, Reece winked. "I'm no spiv, mate. I got a profession. And it ain't hawking tickets. That's a sideline."

It was several months before Reece confided that he was a burglar. Hull was mildly intrigued. He went on seeing the other man even when the show folded and he had no more tickets to sell. The burglar was always alone. He seemed to have no friends. His sex life was with professionals. His greatest pride was in his record of nonarrest.

Once Hull mentioned to Reece that a certain actor-manager took home every Friday a slice of the box-office takings. This money would be undeclared on his income-tax returns. On their next meeting, Reece silently handed over a hundred pounds, which Hull silently pocketed. The matter was never discussed.

Sometime later, Hull came across another snippet of information. While waiting in a film studio to be made up for a crowd-scene part, he heard other extras discussing the news that the movie's producer was in a foul mood today because his manservant had quit just when he was without a burglar-alarm system, the old having been removed, the new not yet arrived. Hull passed the news on to David Reece.

In the papers next day, Hull was aghast to read that during a robbery at the producer's house, his rehired servant had been beaten on the head so severely that he had died. A substantial sum of money had been taken, as well as jewellery and silver.

Hull avoided the places where he might meet Reece. Weeks later, when they did meet by accident, he made it plain he wanted no share of the proceeds. Reece was pleased, not offended. He thought Hull was being generous. He apologised for the fact that there'd be no more "business": he was retiring, buying what he'd always wanted, a place in the country. He insisted on giving the address to Hull, who got away as soon as he could.

Hull had not seen the ex-burglar again—and had thought of him hardly at all—until shortly after getting the idea for Vanetti Affair II.

Leaving the master bedroom, Hull began to prowl around the flat. He told himself he had nothing to worry about in respect of his conjugal property being violated. He kept telling himself this while worrying.

Presently, the tranquilizers began to lighten Hull's burden. His thoughts turned from black to grey. He went into the guest room, lay down, didn't wonder whether or not he was going to sleep, and slept.

In the morning, Hull had regained much of his cheer. But he was not as ebullient as he had been. He wondered at one point: what happened to that excitement?

In most of the newspapers the Vanetti story was third lead, not the expected first. But, Hull thought, there'd been no developments for them to go to town on. Just wait till they got the political-hostage news.

Between answering telephone calls—enquirers, press, cranks, and the police asking if the ransom letter had arrived —Hull went down to the lobby and looked outside. He was depressed to see only four people watching from across the road, and on this side one pimply youth lounging. Returning to the flat, he reminded himself how great he'd looked on TV yesterday.

The cleaning woman was pushing a screaming vacuum cleaner around the living room. Hull paid her off and told her she could go, he'd let her know when he wanted her to come back.

Hull telephoned his agent, George Case, who said in the American accent he had acquired from smoking Camels for thirty years, "Sweetheart, how's every little thing? Any news of that darling girl yet?"

"Never mind the darling girl, what about *me?* Getting anything together workwise? Who's been after me?"

"Well now, Hull, you know how it is, this is a slack period for us all, the production gelt isn't flowing freely these days and you gotta . . ."

George Chase, Hull realised dully, was peddling all his usual excuses for the no-work problem, and these were not usual times. He assured himself, however, that the affair had only just started. Last time, it had been quite a while before the offers had begun to roll in.

After ringing off, Hull set about getting ready to go to the farm. In the bathroom he removed and flushed away the piece of sticking plaster. He could dispense with it now, thus ending the fret of forgetting to take it off when he donned his disguise.

While changing into the suit whose pockets held cap, scarf and glasses, he cheered himself by recalling for demolition all the worries of last night's insomnia. He finished with the Reece-Elsie nag. He scoffed. David Reece had always gone with whores. Being hung-up on them, he would only be interested in sex when it came in the form of trade.

———◆———

Two blocks along from the apartment house in Lancaster Gate, near a corner, stood Jason Galt in white helmet and blue plastic raincoat. The goggles were pushed up.

He had been here thirty minutes, strolling back and forth beside the hired motorcycle propped at the kerb. He was tense. Having checked earlier, he knew the MGB was still in the garage, and he knew that Hull Rainer must be due to appear soon.

Jason noticed that a man was watching him from a drop doorway. Jason was not surprised at the curiosity. He must, he knew, look odd with his impatient pacing.

He made a show of looking at his wristwatch and shaking his head as if in frustration at someone's tardiness. When he looked up again, it was to see the MGB coming out of the basement garage. The car turned this way.

Jason strode to the kerb. He mounted his machine and moved it forward off its leg, which snapped up into place with a sharp crack like a pistol shot.

After switching on, Jason bent to pump a lever and feed the carburetor. He straightened and kicked down on the starter pedal. The engine coughed.

Jason licked his lips and kicked again. The engine caught, coughed, and died.

Flooded the carburetor, he thought urgently. He glanced behind. The sports car was approaching. He could see Hull Rainer at the wheel.

Turning back and lowering the goggles into place over his eyes, he gave the pedal a mighty kick. The engine didn't even throw out a cough.

The MGB drew level. Jason averted his face. This move was instinctive. He knew he must be unrecognizable in the helmet and goggles and coat.

The sports car turned the corner and went from sight.

Jason stretched himself high, then came down on the pedal heavily. The engine caught, coughed, caught again, began to run with a smooth growl.

Sighing, Jason dropped onto the saddle. He engaged gear and swept away from the kerb—and had to swerve fast to avoid a truck he hadn't noticed. The driver yelled, Jason went on.

He arced around the corner. The car was there, a little way ahead. He was separated from it by two other vehicles, which positioning he reckoned to be just right: close enough to be safe, not close enough to draw attention.

He had no real worries about losing Rainer. If stopped by lights he would soon catch up, being able to thread between lanes. If on an open road, he had in the Norton a match for the car's speed.

Jason felt better than he had since hearing of Elsie's abduction. At last he was doing something solid about the problem. He thought he might even have Elsie back within an hour or two.

From behind came the shrill heehaw of an emergency siren. Jason cleared the way for the following vehicle—ambulance, police car or fire truck.

It came abreast. It was a police car, Jason saw. He next saw, with surprise, that its objective was himself. The passenger officer was signalling to him to stop.

Jason's surprise turned to dismay. He wondered if he could risk ignoring the summons, speeding on. Deciding not, he shot into the side and stopped, left his engine running, got off the bike and propped it, strode on to where the police car was coming to a halt.

Jason leaned down to the open passenger window. "What is it?" he said. "I'm in a hurry."

The policeman said, "Aren't we all."

Jason looked ahead. He saw that he wasn't totally out of luck. The MGB had been stopped by a traffic light.

The driver of the patrol car asked, "That motorbike yours?" He, like the other man, was young and pink-faced and didn't suit his look of sternness.

"Rented. I wasn't speeding. But I am in a hurry."

A new voice came from the back seat: "Why?"

Jason pushed up his goggles. "Date with a dolly. Now come on, boys, don't hold me up."

The front passenger asked in a voice which seemed deliberately slow, "Could I see your driving licence, please?"

Quickly, fumbling under the plastic coat, Jason got out his licence and handed it over. He glanced the other way. The traffic light was still red.

Tapping one foot he asked, "What's the problem anyway?"

The man in the back, who was in plainclothes, said, "There doesn't have to be a problem."

"So why'd you stop me?"

"We're nosy."

Jason swallowed a vicious retort. Antagonising the men would be the worst thing he could do.

The officer in the front said, "And the hire company's document, please."

Hissing, Jason delved back under the raincoat, He brought out the pertinent paper and slapped it into the waiting hand. "It's really important that I see this girl, boys. It's not just romance."

Man in the back: "What's her name?"

"Mary. Not that it matters. Are those papers in order?"

"Seem to be," the uniformed man said, still turning licence and document over as if they were strange.

Jason took a look the other way. The light was changing to green. "Okay?" he asked. "Am I free to go?"

The plainclothesman said, "Your mission can't be that urgent."

"I'm late already."

"Maybe you just don't like talking to coppers."

Jason bent lower and looked into the back of the car. He recognised the man at once, but it took another ten seconds to place him. He was the one who had been watching from the shop doorway.

Jason said, "I see."

The man, middle-aged and with a walrus moustache, said, "Oh, *do* you now?"

"Did Wilkinson ask you to keep an eye on me?"

"Who's Wilkinson?"

Jason looked around. The MGB had moved on and was almost gone from view, far ahead in traffic. He turned and said, "Mary Wilkinson."

"That's the girl you're going to see?"

"No. Elsie Vanetti. I've got her tied up in a tower. Follow me if you like." He addressed the uniformed man. "Could I please have my papers back, kind sir, Officer, along with your gracious permission to leave."

Sour-faced, the young policeman handed across the documents. "All right?" he asked with his head turned.

"All right," the man in the back said.

"Lovely." Jason straightened. As he moved away he called, "Give my best to Wilkinson and Bart."

He hurried to the motorcycle, leapt onto the saddle and sped off. He zoomed past the police car and then gave its occupants a rich opportunity by going through the traffic light as it was turning from yellow to red.

At well above the speed limit he cut in and around cars. He kept on the main road, throwing glances along every side turning he passed. There was no sign of the MGB. He went on speeding.

Soon he concluded that Rainer must have turned off somewhere. He left the main road and roared back in the direction he had come on quiet streets.

It was ten minutes before Jason suspected he might have lost the chase, another ten before he knew only luck would help, a final ten before he admitted defeat.

He stopped, switched off, and sat slumped in deep dejection.

---

Hull Rainer, nodding in answer to the forefinger-to-cap salute from the old man, drove past the sentry box and into the alley. He felt better now. Activity was cheering, the disguise felt good, and doing the switch had brought its usual tingle of excitement.

He slid the Ford into traffic and headed west. He went as fast as he considered reasonably safe.

Being already in a western suburb of London, it wasn't long before Hull was passing through the outer edges of the city. He congratulated himself on picking this time of day for his visits to the farm—the quiet patch between noon and evening rushes.

That the time had, in fact, been set by David Reece, this Hull was ignoring. Or trying to. It came to him fleetingly along with the contiguous question of why he was continually having to think of self-boosts.

"Everything's going to be great, Albert," he said aloud. That seemed to clinch matters. He settled down to enjoy the drive.

Soon he was in countryside. Hull liked the lush green but knew he'd die of boredom if he had to live among it. He mused that obviously David Reece had a blind spot somewhere.

The village of Compton Pool was peaceful. Only three people were on the one main street as Hull drove through—now at a cautious, legal speed. If, at this stage and area of the game, he were stopped by the police and forced to identify himself, via his licence, it would give rise to all manner of complications. He had no covering story for being in this locale.

So make one up, he told himself. Get on the boy scout ball and be prepared.

After a moment of thought, Hull said, "You know about my wife, Officer? Of course. Well, an hour ago I got instructions on the telephone to drive out this way on a U that'll bring me back to London. At some point I'll be contacted. Now if you'll please excuse me . . ."

Yes, that would do nicely. And while talking he could push back the cap and take off his glasses. Simple.

Two miles beyond the village, Hull came to a crossroads. On one angle stood a pub, The Jolly Miller, a decrepit building whose thatched roof looked more picturesque than serviceable, like a woman's hat.

Turning at the junction, Hull went along a straight stretch of road which was lined with tall chestnut trees, and which reminded him of highways in France. He made another turn, by a haystack. The lane was narrow but hardtopped. It had sides of dense thorn hedges.

He passed gates. Some were grey with age, rotting their way to the ground, others were sparkling with fresh paint which took away some of the gooey cuteness from the names they bore; some were closed and topped with barbed wire, others were as open as unprofessional smiles.

Hull came to a medium gate. That is, it was old but well coated with paint, the name was reasonable, it was open enough to allow careful passage after a double back-and-fill.

"People're used to seeing the gate open," David Reece had said. "They'd think it funny if I started closing it."

"Then stand it ajar," Hull had said. "At least it'll discourage casual callers."

The mud track beyond the gate wended for five hundred yards before Apple Acres came into view. It was a two-story house and a number of sheds, the buildings formed around a yard of mud and cinders like a miniature village square.

Hull entered at a corner and stopped beside the grey van. The house door opened at once. David Reece came out and over to the MBG, his simian face held in an expression of light welcome.

Reece wore his customary country outfit of riding britches, roll-neck sweater and hacking jacket, all showing signs of greasy use. The note he struck was not so much seedy gentleman farmer, more unemployed animal trainer.

Hull got out of the car. "All still okay?"

"Right as the mail," David Reece said. "You look bleeding awful in that get-up."

"I'm supposed to."

"Want to talk to you about a little thing, but there's no time now. I got to be seen in the village."

"Seemed half dead when I came through."

Reece said, "Not in the pubs. I shan't be long. One pint of beer. The shotgun's on the table, coffee on the stove."

"She's all right?" Hull asked.

"Course. Why shouldn't she be?" Reece nodded and turned toward his van. "See you soon."

Hull went to the house and inside, closing the door. He looked around the room, which was untidy but clean, and thought the ex-burglar must be out of his mind to bury himself here.

A grandfather clock ticked, a fire rustled gently in the old-fashioned iron fireplace, a refrigerator whirred in the kitchen. From outside, absolute silence.

"Jesus," Hull said. "Drive you mad."

Considerably cheered by comparisons, he took off and lay on the centre table his glasses and cap. Without admitting it to himself, he wanted to be minus those unflattering objects should the last thing he desired in the world happen—being seen by Elsie. Hull's vanity knew short steps, no bounds.

He passed through an open door and went down a stunted stairway. The room had crates, sacks of fertilizer, firewood, two dismantled bicycles.

It also had a worm-ridden Welsh dresser in natural wood which stood against the left-hand wall; its shelves held a jumble of tools; its feet were hidden by stacks of newspapers.

As Hull knew, the feet had recently-fixed runners. These made simple the task of swinging the heavy piece of furniture out to reveal the new door, behind which was the old door.

Hull was momentarily struck by the fantasy of the fact that a few feet away was his wife. It seemed impossible. But if a reminder was needed, it came when he noticed a nearby pile of clothes: gumboots, muffler, boilersuit, hat. The ultra-masculine heap was topped off absurdly with a delicate nylon stocking.

Looking at the clothes, Hull was visited by a curious notion. What if he were to get dressed up as the abductor, go in there and see Elsie? He wouldn't do it, of course, but the idea was enough to bring pleasure, an exaggeration of the safety he felt when wearing his own feeble disguise. It was what acting was all about.

He returned to the parlour. Over the following hour he

browsed, glanced warily at the shotgun, poured himself coffee, tended the fire. The same comparisons which had cheered him prevented boredom.

David Reece came back. He slammed the door, dropped a bag of groceries on the table, and went to stand in front of the fire. His eyes were unusually still as he looked down at Hull, who was sprawling in an armchair.

Hull asked, "You wanted to talk to me about something?"

"That's right, mate."

"Go ahead."

Reece said, "There's a little matter you never went into properly about this lark."

"Yes?"

"Why, exactly, you wanted Elsie kidnapped. You mumbled about this and that, but never actually came out with it. Why? What's the reason?"

Hull shrugged. "That really doesn't concern you, Dave. You're being well paid to do an easy job."

"It was easy to pull, yes. Keeping her here is kid's play, yes. But there's the danger of being caught."

"Nonsense. All we—"

Hull broke off as Reece came two swift steps forward and stood over him belligerently. "Don't tell me it's nonsense, mate."

Hull's face twitched in time with the twitches in his heart. "No, Dave. I didn't mean it that way."

"I never use nonsense. Don't give me any more of that crap. You're not talking to a bum, y'know."

"Dave," Hull said earnestly, nervously, "I know I'm not. I'm sorry. I meant it in a friendly way. We're mates, you and I."

Reece stepped back to the hearth. He cleared his throat, shuffled his shoulders and said, "There's the big danger of being caught."

"We've worked all that out, Dave."

"Seeing if Elsie could act? A shock to bring back her memory? She was in it with us for the publicity? No, mate, it's too late for any of that stuff. The first ones might've worked. Not the other. She'd deny it. They'd believe *her*, not us."

"It's a slim chance, us being caught. Just give it a couple of weeks. A thousand pounds isn't bad money."

David Reece showed his crooked teeth. "It's a bloody awful money stood next to half a million dollars."

Hull blinked. "Eh?"

"The money from that last picture."

"Oh."

Reece put his hands on his hips. "Hull," he said firmly and carefully, "you are going to write the ransom note this afternoon, as planned. But it's not going to be about any bloody hostage swap. It's going to ask for two hundred thousand pounds."

Hull gaped at him. "You're out of your mind," he blurted; then, seeing the other man tense, added quickly, "I mean, Elsie doesn't have that kind of money. The Hollywood payment is cut by a third even before it leaves the States."

"Okay. Let's say one hundred thousand."

"No, Dave."

"Yes. Very much yes. And you know why? Because that's what you've been planning all along. A rich killing."

"What?"

"You were going to get a nice ransom out of your wife and give me a cruddy one grand. You didn't plan all this for kicks, Hull boy."

"No—"

"Stop saying no," Reece snapped. "Yes, is the only thing you can say. You have no option."

Dazed, Hull asked, "What d'you mean?"

Reece nodded. He said, "I'm not getting through to you. Listen. You are going to demand one hundred thousand pounds, only half of which you need give to me."

Hull was shaking his head. Reece went on, "Yes. You are going to do it, mate, split me in on your plan, because if you don't I am going to turn Queen's evidence."

Again Hull gaped. His talent for acting had deserted him.

He should have been putting on a scornful performance, calling the bluff. He was too unnerved for anything except a stammered:

"You wouldn't do that."

"Sure I would. Like a shot. As I say, it's too late for fancy stories. If I'm in danger, I want to be well paid for it. You, mate, are going to get me fifty thousand quid. If not, I shop you."

Hull repeated, "You wouldn't do that."

"No? Nothing could be simpler. I just turn real nice with Elsie, tell her all about it and take her with me to the police. You talked me into it, I'd say, which is true enough. I'd have an easy time of it. I don't have a record."

Hull managed to remember, "A wife can't give evidence against her husband."

"Don't know about that. But she can give evidence against me, and I can give evidence against you. Same thing."

"Dave," Hull floundered. "I don't know what to say."

"Yes, that's best. Say nothing." Reece turned to the mantel. He lifted a plastic bag containing a cheap writing pad with matching envelopes, took the bag to the table, put it down and picked up the shotgun. "Start writing. Make the money payable tomorrow night."

Hull stared straight ahead. He was confused. Everything had suddenly turned from cozy to bad. His associate was an enemy. The hostage idea had gone. Vanetti Affair II was going to be a sleazy crime, without even the glamour of immense money; and quick, not spread over several weeks.

"Hull!"

He jerked up to the edge of the seat and looked at the ex-burglar, who was lounging by the door, his gun crooked over his arm. Reece said, "Let's get that letter written. The gloves're there."

Hull got up. That he was afraid of Reece he didn't like to admit, but he did. He couldn't hide it from himself. Nor could he avoid acknowledging the fact that the kidnap idea had been insane in the first place.

Standing by the table he said, "We could call it off now."

David Reece smiled. "Too late." He gestured with the shotgun. "Write that ransom note."

Hull sat down and began to pull on the rubber gloves. He felt small and lost and in need of a kind word. The thought of defying Reece came to him and was hastily discarded. Not for a second did he doubt that the man would go to the police to save himself.

Gloves on, Hull aligned the pad and lifted a ball-point. The wording he would use he already knew by heart. Only the ransom need be changed. Hands unsteady, he printed TO-NIGHT GO TO THE TELEPHONE BOX SOUTH END OF BERKELEY SQUARE AT EIGHT O'CLOCK. WAIT THERE FOR INSTRUCTIONS. BRING WITH YOU ONE HUNDRED THOUSAND POUNDS. DO NOT TELL POLICE. CODE XYZ.

David Reece, who had moved forward to watch, said, "Now the envelope."

Hull addressed an already stamped envelope, using the same ungainly printing. He sealed it with the note inside, and put it in his pocket wrapped in a page from the pad—this so he could handle it later without leaving prints; he didn't know if the police planned on intercepting his mail.

"Okay," Reece said, going back to the fire. "Post it on your way home. You'll get it in the morning. Then draw out the money. Tomorrow night pretend to deliver it. Next day, bring me my share, and we put Elsie back in circulation."

Hull got up and dully pulled off the gloves, put on his glasses and cap. He nodded when Reece said, "See you tomorrow afternoon."

Twenty minutes later Hull parked the car in Chiswick. He mailed the letter and walked on toward a telephone both. He sighed in dreariness. All his planning and work, and the result was a four-and-a-half day wonder that would be forgotten in two and a quarter days. Not only that, but if he didn't dance well to Reece's tune he could be in real trouble.

In the call box he dialled the number of Elsie's agent.

Minnie Brent was a thin woman who smiled all the time except when near Hull Rainer, whom she despised. The feeling was mutual. They had always gone to great lengths to avoid each other.

When connected, Hull asked without preamble, "That money arrive from the Coast yet?"

"On my desk right now."

"Good. Pay into Elsie's and my joint account."

"Like hell I will," Minnie Brent said. "I'll wait for instructions from my client."

"Your client, it may have escaped your narrow notice, is being held prisoner. To get her free I need money. Without it she could be killed."

"I doubt that."

"You," Hull said, "would doubt your own grandmother. Get that money into the account. Soonest. If you don't, I'll pull out all stops to see that Elsie kicks you free and gets a new agent. Do you read me clear?"

"And very, very loud."

"The money?"

After a pause, Minnie Brent said a blunt, "Will do." The line went dead.

Hull left the telephone booth and walked in a slump back to his car. He had never in his life felt so wretched.

———◄━►———

Elsie hummed cheerfully. She had forced herself to a form of determined euphoria after realising that her worst enemy was depression. She had filled the long, otherwise empty afternoon with physical action which itself would result in physical comfort.

First she had taken the chill off water by balancing the basin atop the electric fire. In the water she had washed her panties and bra. These had taken an hour to dry in front of the red bars, during which time she had heated more water.

Finding a washcloth had been an interesting problem. She had considered the cuff of her cardigan and a swatch cut from the lining of her coat, before settling on the towel as source.

With her teeth she had worked on a corner until she freed a piece six inches square.

Stripping first to the waist, next from the waist down, Elsie had bathed. It had done wonders for her spirits. She had decided that from now on she would keep herself clean and occupied, even if the latter only meant endlessly making and unmaking the bed.

Humming, Elsie strode a circle around the dirt floor. She was managing to dismiss the knowledge that her hair was a tangly mess.

At the expected time, the key grated in the lock, the door opened and the man entered with a tray of food. Elsie would not have been able to say why, but she sensed in the guard a different attitude. He seemed, like herself, more cheerful.

Door locked, tray slid on the table, he moved off to lean against the wall. No word had been exchanged as yet. Elsie sat and gave her attention to the canned spaghetti, bread, shop-cake and milk.

"Thought I'd do you that spaghetti as a treat," the man said. "I know what you Eyetalians are for your pasta."

Elsie was musing while she ate that although she wouldn't be able to identify her guard, undisguised, she would never forget his voice, the accent, the mannerisms and the timbre. But she told herself it could be assumed, phony.

She said, "It was kind of you. Thanks."

"Note also I brought you some dessert. That cake."

"Thank you very much."

"That's okay. Just don't mention it to the other boys, that's all."

Elsie asked, "Will I see them?"

"Maybe not."

"How many of you are there?"

He said, "Listen, dearie. No questions, eh? Don't ask me no questions and you'll get no lies."

"All right."

Elsie finished her meal in silence. Standing, she leaned back against the table. She asked, "What shall I call you?—if that's a question I'm allowed to ask."

"Call me Joe, if you like."

"It's not your name, of course."

"Of course. Neither me nor the other five have names."

That, Elsie thought, was a deliberate slip, a calculated leak. It meant little—except it was certain that six was not the right number.

The man tapped a side pocket of his boilersuit. "Got something in here I believe you'd like."

"What is it?"

"Books. Couple of paperbacks. Best-sellers they were."

Knowing his sense of humour, Elsie said, "Show me."

He eased into view the corner of a book, pushed it back. "Real interesting stuff. Spy stories. Takes you away from your troubles, a good read."

"Are you going to let me have them?"

"Well now," he said, folding his arms and crossing his legs at the ankles. "I don't know about that."

"You must, otherwise you wouldn't have mentioned it."

He nodded. "Tell you what, dearie. I'll give you these books in exchange for a little kiss. It's not the kiss itself I'm bothered about. See, I want to be able to say I kissed the famous Elsie Vanetti."

"You'd give yourself away if you did," Elsie said, trying to keep it light. "You'd be caught."

"I'd only tell the right ones."

"And if you wanted to kiss me, I'd see your face."

He shook his head. "Not if I was real close. Shall I show you how?"

Elsie looked away, giving one shoulder a lift-drop. That seemed the best way of answering in the affirmative, which is what she wanted.

Before the mention of books, she had been relatively content. Now her need of reading matter was desperate. If she could stand him kissing her, she saw no reason why she shouldn't go through with it. A kiss was harmless enough.

The man stopped beside her. He moved again, moved until he was pressing close. Elsie didn't avoid the contact, though she did keep her face turned the other way. She felt his left arm come lightly around her shoulders, glimpsed his right arm go up as he reached toward the stocking mask.

"Okay," he said softly, and she could feel the heat of his breath on her cheek. "Turn this way with your eyes closed."

She obeyed. Eyelids firmly down, which helped a great deal, she turned her head. She surprised herself by thinking, This is Jason.

The man's mouth settled on her lips, his arm pressed, the other arm went around her waist, he eased his body closer. Elsie tried to concentrate on the fact that the stocking top, pushed up to uncover the lower face, was nuzzling her cheek.

The man was gently moving and shaping her lips with his own. He probed with his tongue, meeting her teeth. She shuddered, prickled all over with a heat which she told herself was embarrassment, and kept her teeth clenched.

She thought swirlingly of reading, of the last book she had read, of a film about spies she had seen last week on television.

The man was embracing her closely, warmly. She felt wanted. She was with another human being. His mouth was caressing her lips as if they were precious. His tongue importuned again.

Jason, Elsie thought as she slowly allowed access. The heat of her body increased with each movement of his tongue. When those movements became rhythmic she decided she was disgusted and could stand it no more.

Elsie turned her head away to free her mouth. "Enough," she gasped. "One kiss."

The man said in a low, sly voice, "I was only just getting warmed up."

She drew out of his embrace and moved over to the wall. "You've had your kiss." Her heartbeat was erratic. She turned to see him pulling the stocking under his chin.

"It wasn't a real long one, dearie."

"Longer than average."

He gave a laugh-snort which sounded amiable. "Okay. A deal's a deal." He worked the two books out of his pocket and tossed them on the table. "There you go."

"Thanks."

"You don't regret the bargain, do you?"

Elsie said, "I think I'll read now. If you'll excuse me."

The man went to the door, where he paused. He asked, "Like to know what I've got in this other pocket?"

Elsie wanted to reply in the negative. She couldn't help saying, "What?"

"A comb, dearie."

Elsie closed her eyes to help the fight. She said, "I think I'll read my books now."

"Lovely comb. Good and strong. Expensive."

"If you'll excuse me."

Heavily, the man gave a mock sigh. "Oh, well. Maybe another time. Goodnight."

Elsie didn't open her eyes or relax the grip on herself until she heard the door close behind the guard. Then she stalked to the corner to spit.

———◆———

It was one o'clock in the morning. Jason was exhausted. He was also so cold that his fingers and toes were numb. A recent and sudden shower had caught him before he could reach shelter, plastering his hair to his head—with the arrival of darkness he had taken off the crash helmet.

As stamping and clapping would make too much noise in the silent desertion, Jason contented himself with rubbing his hands together as he paced a strip of sidewalk in Lancaster Gate. The wet, hunched figure was a far cry from the man who once had worn white tie and tails nightly.

Jason became interested in hypnotism during his first year in medical school. At about the same time he joined the university's drama group and fell in love with theatricals. These two, the science and the art, were to remain the guiding influences of his life.

What time Jason had to spare from studying hypnotism, he spent in playing at being an actor. It came as no surprise when one of his professors told him he was wasting his time in general medicine. Jason quit school.

For a year he studied with a hypnotist in London, then for eighteen months with a hypnotherapist in Vienna. On returning to England he found everyone was talking about a stage hypnotist playing the Palladium, and saw how to bring together his two loves in a marriage that would be highly satisfying as well as profitable.

Jason worked out an act, got work in small clubs, prospered gradually over the years, finished at the top of his particular ladder by touring provincial music halls as headliner. For two seasons all was fine. Then new laws banned all stage demonstrations of hypnotism because some people had suffered dangerous after-effects. From then on, Jason spent a decade of aimless drifting—bit-player work here, hypnotherapy there—until he got the idea which came to be called the Vanetti Affair, and which eventually led to him being on a Lancaster Gate street in the wet, cold, early hours of the morning.

Jason looked at his wristwatch. Realising he had been in this area for more than twelve hours, he felt doubly exhausted.

After losing Hull Rainer, Jason had decided that the day wouldn't be totally wasted if he were to establish more accurately the time of the actor's return from his mysterious outing.

Jason had driven back to the vicinity of the Vanetti-Rainer apartment house to wait. Some of the time he was able to spend in the warmth of a pub, watching from a window. Rainer returned in his MGB at close to four o'clock.

Jason had got a new idea. He went in the basement garage and over to the sports car. He peered inside. Despite the extra dimness, he was able to read, and make note of, the MGB's mileage. Now, should he again fail to follow the actor tomorrow, he would at least know how far he had travelled.

Since then, on the chance of Rainer going out again, Jason had continued his watch—in the street until the pubs opened, from the bar window until closing time, back in the street, with regular and quick trips around onto Bayswater Road to look up at the windows of the flat.

On his last check there, the lights had gone out, sending Jason hurrying back to watch the building's door and garage. Hull Rainer had not appeared. Now half an hour had passed and Jason decided he could call off the watch.

He went stiffly to his motorcycle, got on, started the engine and drove away. His chill increased as the air charged at him. The pity he felt was not for himself but for Elsie.

———————————

Hull said, "Good morning, Inspector. Rainer here."

Wilkinson's voice over the telephone line was as void of expression as his face: "Morning, sir. I take it there's been a development."

"Yes. It's arrived. The ransom demand."

"You opened it?"

Hull said, "Yes, but not to worry, I used eyebrow tweezers to get the paper out. I remembered about smudging possible fingerprints."

"Good. And the contents, please?"

"They want a hundred thousand pounds," Jason said. "It has to be delivered tonight."

"That doesn't give us much time," Wilkinson said briskly. "We'll have to work fast. I'll be over there in fifteen minutes."

Hull said, "No. Hold on. I don't want you to come here."

"What?"

"Listen. Meet me in half an hour. Let's make it the coffee shop downstairs in Whitely's. I'll explain when I see you."

"I don't understand."

"You will, Inspector," Hull said. "Goodbye for now."

He put down the receiver and went morosely into the

kitchen, where he poured a post-breakfast cup of tea. He drank it standing at the sink while looking with resentful eyes at the newspapers spread on the table.

Vanetti Affair II had been relegated to the second page, and there dealt with briefly. Hull came close to a feeling of understanding. He was losing interest himself. His greatest wish now was to be safe. The celebrity profit he had hoped for had become a minor aim. He was not even overly concerned that *Time* magazine's man had failed to show up yesterday.

Tea finished, Hull added the cup to the pile of unwashed crockery and went through to his bedroom. He put on a beret, sunglasses and a duffel coat, which outfit he usually liked for its hint of movie-star-on-location. Today he was unlifted.

The telephone rang as he was going out of the flat. With a tut of annoyance Hull went back to answer. He hoped vaguely that it was someone he could shout at.

The caller was Andrew Wilson of *Time,* apologising for failing to keep his appointment. "There was that fire in Wapping I had to cover. Sorry."

Hull's "That's okay" was the verbal version of a shrug of indifference.

"But I'm free today for lunch, if you can make it, between twelve and two."

"Busy. Four o'clock? Five?"

They settled on four. Hull disconnected, left the flat and went downstairs.

The morning was grey. A drizzle fell steadily. There were no people on the street—no reporters, no gawkers. Sighing, Hull trudged off toward Queensway.

The nearby shopping thoroughfare was dominated by Whitely's, a department store which looked as if it had just run away from Oxford Street. Hull crossed the road to the pillared entrance. Inside was warm and bright, but it didn't help. He threaded stands and passed under a curving stairway.

The counter area smelled of coffee, the people sitting and standing there smelled of damp clothes and cough lozenges.

Standing aside and alone was Chief Inspector Harold Wilkinson. He saw Hull, and started to approach.

Hull jerked his head and walked on. He went a dozen yards to the book department, rounded a stack of shelves which acted as a screen and stopped there. The policeman joined him, his eyebrows raised a quarter inch.

Hull said, "I don't think I was followed."

"Followed? By whom?"

Hull looked both ways. "I mustn't be seen talking to you."

"Mr. Rainer," Wilkinson said. "Would you mind telling me what this is in aid of."

"Here's the letter. Read it."

He took the envelope without caution, but used the extreme points of finger and thumb to extract the note. He scanned it rapidly. "Yes. Okay. I'll keep this, if you don't mind."

"Sure. That's why I brought it. The prints. If it weren't for that I would've burned it. Or anyway, kept it from you till this thing was over."

"Why is that, sir?"

"You've read the letter," Hull said. "I'm not supposed to tell the police. That means my wife could be hurt unless I play along. And that's precisely what I intend doing."

Wilkinson put the letter in his pocket. "You're going to pay?"

"Of course. That goes without saying. What does have to be said is this. I want you to stay out of it completely."

"Can't do that, sir."

Hull said, "Listen, Inspector. My wife's life could be at stake." He winced at the dialogue. "I don't care about the niceties of the law. I care about Elsie."

"We have a job to do, sir."

"Well, I don't suppose I can stop you from following me, but I won't lift a finger to help you. Not until I've got my wife back."

"We could arrange a trap very easily."

"No."

"We could have the money treated with chemicals."

"No."

"I could, you know, charge you with obstruction."

"Be my guest."

Chief Inspector Wilkinson got out his pipe and looked into the bowl with one eye closed. "So you plan on going to that telephone booth by yourself, eh?"

"Right. Just me and the money."

"Well, we'll have a tap on it. We'll get the message at the same time you do."

"So be it."

"Not, however, that it means a fat lot. I doubt if you'll be told to go directly to a delivery point. You'll be sent to another booth, and then another."

"No doubt the bastards will lead me a merry dance."

The policeman looked up. "And no doubt we'll be close behind every inch of the way. So you might as well work with us."

Hull shook his head. "Sorry. I've given you the letter. That's all I'll do till I've got Elsie back safely. Afterwards it'll be a different matter."

"Which bank do you use, Mr. Rainer?"

"Sorry. I have nothing more to tell you."

Wilkinson tapped the bite of his pipe against his bottom teeth, which, Hull was offended to see, were perfect in form and whiteness. The policeman said:

"All right, sir. But I have something I can tell you. About the investigation. It's been quite ill but has now taken a slight turn for the better."

Hull tightened his legs. "Oh?" He was glad he had on the sunglasses.

"We think we know what kind of vehicle was used in the abduction. It was seen leaving the basement garage at the pertinent time. Last night and this morning we checked with everyone in the building. The vehicle's unknown."

"What—um—kind is it?"

"A van. Small grey van."

"I see."

"Make unknown—which is natural enough, since the witness is a female nondriver. She was on the other side of the street, waiting for a cab that was coming to take her to the airport. She had a package-deal two days in Paris, and didn't hear about Miss Vanetti till she was on the plane coming back."

"Could the van," Hull said carefully, "have belonged to a workman? Plumber or something?"

Wilkinson shook his head. "Checked that out too, of course. No work's been done in the building. There were no deliveries, no pick-ups."

Hull made himself smile. "Well, Inspector, this looks pretty good. It's a sound lead, seems to me." He was relieved when the policeman put his pipe away with what looked like despondency.

"Our traffic department tells me only about half a million vehicles fit that description."

"My God."

"But we're working on it. We've had slimmer clues. The back-street garages might tell us something—respray job, y'know, or removal of a false grey finish."

"Yes, that might do it," Hull droned.

"After we've worked on it ourselves we'll give it to the press, see what the public can come up with. The gang might've made a slip somewhere."

"Sounds as if you think this was a cleverly planned job."

"I do."

Hull felt a fool for feeling proud. But it was better than feeling scared. He said, "Well, I wish you luck, Inspector."

"And me you, Mr. Rainer. I promise we'll keep in the background tonight, and if you change your mind about working with us—give me a ring."

Hull nodded, turned, left. He strode toward the front of the store, veered off course near the entrance and went into the men's clothing department. He finished up back near the coffee-shop counter. At a cowl telephone he got his bank's number from the book, dialled and asked for the manager.

"Good morning. Hull Rainer speaking. I'll be calling around presently and I wonder if you could have a sum of money ready for me. It's in connexion with something you've probably heard about."

"Ah yes," the man said slowly. "Yes, indeed, Mr. Rainer. What sum did you have in mind?"

"One hundred thousand pounds."

"Very good, sir. Any particular make-up? We can give you a thousand notes of a hundred, or ten thousand tens."

"Better make it half and half. Thank you. I'll be there in a few minutes."

Next, Hull headed for the luggage department. He had no need to go that far, he saw, passing the stationery counter. It had attaché cases in simulated leather which would suit his purpose. He bought one, left the store and went along the street.

Hull was recovering from his early depression and from Wilkinson's information re the van (half a million, eh?). So much so that, before going into the bank, he took off his sunglasses and beret in order for the view of him to be unobstructed. Entering the place with a flourish, he then spent an enjoyable five minutes writing a check, having the case filled with crisp notes, and being looked at by staff and customers.

Hull strode home. In the living room he opened his case and let the money tumble onto the table. Looking at the lovely pile of wads, he smiled. He realised what worry had previously kept back, that half of this was for himself. He was feeling better and better. He thought that if he dare risk it, if he dare tell Reece he'd been able to raise only fifty grand, he would have a splendid seventy-five thousand pounds.

Hull knelt, still smiling, and began to build a tower with the wads of money. When it fell down he started on construction of a house. He played happily.

---

Elsie was combing her hair.

The man in the stocking mask, perched on the table, swung

his legs complacently. He glanced down at the soup and coffee on the tray beside him: "This lunch is going to get cold."

"I'll have it later," Elsie said. She was sitting on the straight chair, which she had brought here and set beside the fire, opposite the table.

The man folded his arms. "I bet you been combing away ever since this morning."

She wondered when he was going to leave. "I have."

"Feels good, eh?"

"Yes."

"Earning the comb felt good too, didn't it?"

She ignored him. She didn't care to remember. She thought how nice it would be to wash her hair in masses of hot sudsy water.

"Felt good for me," the man said, a mocking tone in his voice. "I don't mind admitting it. I liked putting my hand under your sweater."

"All right."

"And then sliding my hand up real slow and making you shiver."

Elsie said, "Forget it." Brutally she yanked the comb through a tangled knot.

"Yes, very enjoyable," the man said. He was still swinging his legs. "Worked for you too, I'll bet. Don't know why you had to move away."

Elsie ran the comb gently down a hank of hair. "A deal's a deal. You said so yourself."

"Maybe we can make a new deal."

She lowered the comb and looked at him steadily. "Doesn't repetition bore you?"

"It don't have to be the same thing, dearie."

"Logical progression, you mean?"

"Yeah, that's right."

As if musing aloud, Elsie said, "It would be nice to have some hot water. Lots of it."

The man seemed to be returning her steady gaze. Slowly he

stopped swinging his legs. "Hot water," he said. "That could be arranged."

"Six books."

"Yes, can do."

"Paper and pencil," Elsie said.

"I've got paper and pencil."

They were both perfectly still, both speaking quietly. Elsie said, "A piece of carpet to cover this dirt."

"Yes, there is a rug I could bring in."

"Another blanket."

"Yes."

Looking down, Elsie tapped the comb in the palm of her hand. "I can't think of anything else."

"That's quite a lot," the man said. "Hot water, books, writing material, rug, blanket. Hell of a lot."

She shook her head. "Not for the limit," she said, looking at him carefully. "Not for everything."

The man unfolded his arms. He reached down and gripped the edge of the table. He said softly, "A radio."

Elsie's tapping became busier. The man went on, "A portable radio, and all them other things, in exchange for you and me in bed together. Now. Right now."

Elsie stopped tapping. Do it, she told herself. You can do it. You're braver than you think.

Her voice was tight as she asked, "How long for?"

"Half an hour."

She shook her head again. "Too long."

"Fifteen minutes."

She gave a small nod. "Okay."

"That's a sensible girl."

"You won't back out of the bargain afterwards?"

"A deal's a deal," he said.

Elsie rose and put her comb on the chair. "I'd prefer to have the light off."

"Can't do that."

She walked awkwardly to the bed. Her back to the man,

she took off the cardigan and threw it on the bed. Quickly she pulled the top over her head and took off the skirt.

Go on, she ordered herself. Too late to stop. You're as good as nude already.

Elsie put her hands behind. She unhooked the bra and tossed it with the other garments. She put both hands to her waist, and hesitated.

There was perfect silence in the room. Then, as she listened while hesitating, still wondering if she could go through with it, she heard the man's breathing. It was even and deep.

Elsie put her fingers inside the elastic, pushed down. Her briefs dropped. She stooped swiftly, picked them up, threw them on the bed.

She commanded herself to turn. This, she thought consolingly, was the worst part, and would be over quickly, and she could pretend she was wearing a bikini.

But Elsie was unable to pretend, to switch her mind away, as she turned to face the man. She kept her eyes lowered. A blush heated her face.

There was a creak of wood as the man got off the table, a padding of his footsteps as he came toward her. His boots appeared in her curtailed vision. She looked up. She was glad she couldn't see his face.

"Get undressed quickly," she whispered. "It's cold." That stated fact enabled her to huddle, to fold her arms across her breasts and coveringly raise one leg.

The man stopped four feet away. With swift movements he pulled a zipper down from neck to waist and began to shuck the one-piece garment off his shoulders.

The moment had come. Elsie's nerves started to race. You can do it, she insisted to herself urgently. You must do it. And now. Now!

She threw herself forward.

With a cry of hate and fear and hope, she struck the man in the chest with her fists and sent him staggering. In his attempt at maintaining balance he twisted around. Elsie grabbed the back of the boilersuit and jerked it lower, further imprisoning his arms.

He gave a strangled cry of, "Bitch!"

She stepped in close and embraced him from behind. Her right hand dove into his pocket. Her fingers touched the large key. Then she whipped her hand out empty as she felt herself falling.

The man had thrown himself backwards. They landed on the floor. Elsie was underneath. The air had been driven from her lungs. She fought to breathe while the man kicked and rocked to free himself.

Elsie held on tightly with both arms. Apart from gasps, she and the man were silent. His elbows battered her ribs, his head scuffled against her face, his boots thudded against her ankles and shins.

Abruptly, the man went still. He drew his head far forward. Just in time, before he flung it back, Elsie realised he was going to do so. She twisted away. The back of his head thumped against her shoulder.

Her breathing was better. As the man began again on his twisting and kicking, she thrust her hand back in his pocket. She grasped the key, drew it out, and then tried to fling the man aside.

"No you don't," he grated. He spread his feet and held the upper position.

Swinging with all her strength, she moved him right, left, right again. The feet pushed him back every time.

She sent her left hand lower on the boilersuit, reaching for the man's crotch. At once his knees shot up in protection. She swung him mightily to the side. He rolled off.

Elsie jumped up. She leapt at the door. She stammered the key on the metal around the lock. A staccato moan nagged from her slack lips. She glanced behind.

The man was upright from his knees, fighting the boilersuit forward onto his shoulders. He seemed to be hindered by too much clothing.

Elsie got the key in the lock. She twisted it. There was no

turn, no give. She tried the other way. The key went, the lock clicked open.

The man snarled. He was on his feet, arms freed, running toward her with grappling hands.

Elsie doubled up. The move was involuntary, like a child avoiding a slap. Her shoulder caught the man in the stomach. He gasped and careened to the wall. Elsie straightened. She grabbed the door and jerked it open.

The other door was open already: a shaft of space. She flung herself into it and felt a hand from behind clutch at her shoulder. A pile of newspapers tripped her up.

She went sprawling, fell on hands and knees. The doors boomed: the man was crashing through.

Elsie leapt up. She was in a storeroom. There was a short flight of steps leading to a doorway. She raced there. The man's pounding footfalls seemed to be right at her back. She took the steps in one leap.

Naked apart from her shoes, and giving no thought to the fact, Elsie burst into a parlour. That it was void of life neither gladdened nor surprised her. She hadn't stopped to consider the other gang members. Her first and only idea had been escape from the room.

Stage two was now. Escape from the house.

Elsie reached the door. She turned the handle and pulled. There was no response. She saw the heavy bolt. Before her hand could go to it, the man was upon her.

She stepped back and aside while ducking. The man's embrace of capture, fast as a jaw-snap, missed her narrowly.

Elsie slipped around to the other side of the centre table. She stood there in a crouch, arms out, ready to dodge either way. Her chest heaved, her breasts swung, her face trembled. She was too unnerved to feel fear.

Beyond the table barrier, the man was in a similar pose. His breathing was loud, raspy. Hat gone, the leg of the stocking hung foolishly like a trick pigtail.

He made a lunge to the left, stopped abruptly and went the

other way. Elsie had been fooled by the first move. The gap between hunted and hunter was short as they raced around the table.

One of the chair backs caught Elsie's hand. She grasped and jerked. The chair flew back from its place and fell. The man leapt it without trouble.

Elsie made another full circuit. She picked up the chair, swinging it high. The man paused in his rush. Elsie swung the chair around her head, and flung it at the window.

She missed. The chair hit the wall and bounced off. It clattered back and struck her on the leg.

Again Elsie and the man were in crouching stalemate one on either side of the table. Less than one minute had elapsed since they had been in the parlour.

With a jerk of his head which seemed to signify sudden recollection, the man leaned forward. He directed his face toward the tabletop. Among the flotsam lay a shotgun.

Elsie made a grab. The man did the same. The race was a draw. Their hands fumbled and squabbled for possession. The stronger pair won.

Elsie had turned away before the enemy had lifted his gun from the table. Her eyes, wild, saw a part-open door in a corner. Through it showed a climbing staircase.

She darted there.

The man barked, "Stop or I shoot!"

Elsie reached the door, clattered through, fought up the steep and narrow stairs. The man was behind her at once. His fingers raked her ankle.

She came to the upper level. It was a tiny hall. Three doors fed from it, all open. She made her choice, entered a bedroom, slammed the door behind her, reached for whatever locking device might be there. None was there.

The door burst inward. Elsie swung around and away. The window, she saw, was open. She leapt on the bed, off the bed, arrived at the window and leaned out. She screamed.

Her hair was grabbed, pulled viciously. She had to follow.

The blow caught her on the side of the head. She was knocked away from the window and spun around. The man's next punch she saw coming but was unable to act.

Her jaw exploded with pain. Everything in her vision broke up into fragments and then dissolved into a jiggling greyness. She felt herself falling. Next, she was being half-dragged, half-carried. Her feet bounced down steps. The greyness deepened into black.

Elsie found herself blinking in protection against brightness. She recognised it for the bulb in the cellar. Eyes braver, she saw in one swoop that she was lying on the bed, that her hands and feet were tied each to a corner, that at the bedfoot the man was standing and staring at her spreadeagled nakedness.

She turned her head to the side. Her jaw ached. She mumbled, "Don't look at me."

"Think yourself lucky you're alive."

"Thanks. Thanks for not shooting."

The man said, "You can pay me back by not mentioning this to the other boys."

"Yes."

"They might've heard you. Then you'd have been in real trouble. They're not as easy as I am. You were bloody stupid."

"Yes," she said. "Please stop looking at me."

"You're nice to look at."

"Do it. Get it over with."

The man asked, "Do what, dearie?"

"You know."

"No, thanks."

She turned her head. "What?"

"Listen," the man said. "Rape's not my cup of tea. I don't want it this way. I can be a lot of help to you if you'll just see reason. You think about that."

He moved forward and out of sight behind her head. The next moment she felt her right wrist being freed and heard, "You can untie the rest yourself. See you later."

The door closed with a slam.

To hide her nakedness and despair, Elsie put her hand over her eyes.

———————⚫◆▶——————

The MGB came out of the basement garage.

Jason was ready. Helmet on, goggles in place, he sat astride his motorcycle, the engine of which was idling.

Rather than risk an uncertain start, Jason had spent the past thirty minutes patrolling the street between bouts of standing. He had watched particularly for the plainclothes detective of yesterday, without seeing him.

The sports car approached, came level, passed and went on to the corner, which it turned. Jason found the repetition comforting.

He followed at a cautious distance. He was more worried about police interference than losing or being seen by Hull Rainer. But it was a small worry. He felt confident.

The traffic lights were on green. The MGB went through, trailed by a furniture van, trailed by the motorcycle.

Jason was all set for a journey of some consequence. Surprise and doubt took him when, five minutes after leaving Lancaster Gate, Hull Rainer turned off into a side street and came to a stop by a church.

Jason kept going forward. It seemed the safer, less suspicious, of the alternatives, others being a halt or a turn. He passed within a yard of the actor as he was getting out of his car.

Stopping fifty feet on, in front of a house, Jason pretended for effect, in case Rainer was watching, to wave at someone in an upper window. He looked back.

The actor was walking this way.

Jason's indecision lasted five seconds. He left the engine ticking over, got off the bike and went through the house gateway. Although he doubted if Rainer would recognise him from his build and the bottom part of his face, he wasn't about to take chances.

The actor was twenty feet away, walking briskly. He glanced at houses, glanced at Jason, glanced at a woman pushing a baby carriage.

Jason stopped at the house door. He went through the motions of ringing the bell without actually touching it. He listened to the footfalls from behind.

It occurred to him, insanely, that this might be where Hull Rainer was headed. If so, what would he do? It occurred to him also, sensibly, that it was encouragingly odd for Rainer to be on foot when there was parking space galore.

Against the mottled glass in the door's top half, a face appeared. It pressed there grotesquely. A shrill female voice asked, "What is it?"

Jason didn't answer. He kept still.

Hull Rainer was abreast now. The woman called, "What do you want?"

Jason pressed the bell. It rang loudly. The face jumped away from the glass, came back and was joined by two flattened hands. The voice shrilled, "What *is* it?"

Rainer had gone by.

Jason turned and went along the path. He mounted his motorcycle and sat watching the other man. The house door opened. A face peered out. At a corner, Rainer paused and looked back.

Jason raised a thoughtful-seeming hand to his chin. Whether or not it made any difference he didn't know. What mattered was that Hull Rainer continued, went from sight.

Jason waved at the woman, engaged gear, moved on. He wheeled slowly to the corner and rounded it with care. The actor was well ahead. Jason followed, dawdling his machine and letting its engine tick over quietly. He kept behind parked cars whenever possible.

After several blocks a shopping district appeared. The sidewalks were crowded. Jason began to close the gap. It was down to twenty feet by the time Hull Rainer joined the shoppers.

There was traffic here. Jason had to move with care. He

divided his attention between the road and his prey. He reduced the gap to a dangerous ten feet.

Turning from watching a car go by, Jason thought for a sickening moment that he had lost the actor. Then he saw him. He was going into a Woolworth's.

Quickly steering to a nose-on stand between two parked cars, Jason switched off and propped the machine. He hurried between passers-by, went through the swing doors. Hull Rainer was strolling toward the rear. Jason followed.

He was still unsure, doubtful. On one hand, Rainer parking the car such a distance from the shops was curious, unless his desire had been for an aimless walk away from the tensions at home. On the other hand, browsing in Woolworth's was not at all out of the ordinary.

Hull Rainer moved politely through the people. He changed aisles, got to the side, reached the corner. He went into a doorway marked WASHROOMS.

Jason approached cautiously. He looked into the gloom of a passage and saw two doors, one for each sex, distinguished for the sake of foreign tourists by a pipe on one and a bonnet on the other.

Jason turned away. He went to the nearest counter. A girl there looked at him expectantly. He shook his head. The seconds ticked by. He began to feel nervous.

Swinging around he went over to the passage and inside. He put a hiding hand to his chin as he opened the pipe door. The room had two stalls. Both were empty.

Jason backed off in a rush. He noticed now a third door. He strode to it, pushed, and found himself in a backyard. He ran across it and out into an alley. The alley was deserted.

Jason took a chance and ran to the left. He came to a corner, turned it, and was in a cul-de-sac. He ran back the other way.

The street he arrived on was quiet. Over the way stood a line of taxies. There was no sign of Hull Rainer.

Jason, his nerves scratching, decided his goal must be one of the gates along the alley. He was about to turn back when the first cab in line pulled away and a face looked through the side window.

Despite a cap and glasses, Jason recognised the actor. He recognised him and felt awed. He stared after the departing taxi. A thrill zigzagged his belly and chest. His doubt went. He knew he had been right all along. Car-store-taxi plus a disguise, Hull Rainer had to be in it up to his pampered hair.

Jason snapped alert. He read off the cab's licence number and kept repeating it as he ran to the main street and along to his motorcycle.

He unpropped the machine, kicked it to life, made a roaring U-turn almost under the wheels of a bus, cut dangerously in front of another vehicle, and got into the side road.

The cab was nowhere in sight. Jason drove at top speed, his raincoat flapping and slapping like an enraged weakling. Street after street went by.

Jason passed a turning, thought he had glimpsed a black shape in its far distance, braked and arced around. He went into the road and sped on.

Yes, the shape was a taxi. And yes, the number was right. Heating up with relief, Jason reduced speed.

Soon, in the middle of a long street, the cab's stoplights flashed on. Jason stopped first, pulling into the side and safely out of view behind a truck. He dismounted and peered along the avenue.

Hull Rainer paid the fare and started walking. The cab left. Jason waited until the actor was well ahead before pulling out on his motorcycle to follow. It was not for long. The man in front turned into a lane beside a cinema.

When Jason reached that point, he stopped. He was uncertain of his next move. Should he follow on foot or driving, or not follow at all?

He felt sure there was no way out from behind the movie house, that the lane didn't go through to another street. What was most likely, he thought on noticing a sign which said PARKING AT REAR, was that Rainer had a car planted back there.

So when Jason heard the sound of a motor growing from along the lane, he turned and steered behind the nearest vehicle and crouched low. A car came out, a green Ford. At the wheel was Hull Rainer.

With that zigzag of thrill again, part of it caused by his having guessed right, Jason warily moved out of cover and followed.

Fifteen minutes later they were in countryside. The Ford lay an eighth of a mile ahead and was separated from Jason by a bus. Constantly he swept to one corner or the other of the broad vehicle to check on Rainer.

They came to a village. Signs indicated it was called Compton Pool. There were few people about. The bus came to a slow stop. Jason went past it cautiously, but speeded up when he glimpsed the Ford just going out of sight ahead.

The road beyond the village was a series of bends. The Ford moved in and out of view. Jason felt confident. He didn't fuss when he was forced to crawl momentarily behind a tractor.

Free again, he raced ahead. One long, swooping bend brought him in sight of a crossroads. There was no sign of the green Ford. Cursing his confidence, Jason slowed at the junction and looked along the arms. He saw nothing. There was no one around to ask which way the car had gone. The pub on a corner, no one was watching from its windows.

Left, right or straight on? Jason couldn't make up his mind and he was wasting precious time. He decided on right solely because the last decision, left behind Woolworth's, had been wrong.

He drove as fast as the road would allow. On either side were lanes and gates. Any one could have been taken by Hull Rainer—if, in fact, he had come this way.

Jason covered five fast miles before realising he would have caught up to the Ford by now. It had either turned off or gone on one of the other roads. And, it suddenly occurred to Jason, the best way to settle direction was to wait at the junction for Rainer's return.

Jason swung around, shoe-scraping the road, and went racing back. At the crossroads he parked beside the pub, which, he saw, was called The Jolly Miller. He went in, pushing up his goggles. His hands were numb with the cold; before, he had been too excited to notice.

Apart from two men playing darts, the place was deserted. Jason leaned on the bar, his ears cocked for car sounds from outside. One of the players came to fill his order of a pint of bitters.

Paying, Jason asked, "Do you know a man called Carson, drives a green Ford? I'm looking for him and I've lost his address."

The man shook his head. "Carson, no. D'you know any Carson, Bill?" The other man didn't know either.

Jason said, "About thirty-five, specs and a cap. Green Ford." The men still didn't know. They went back to their game.

Jason took his beer to a window seat. He was not despondent. He felt pretty sure, from the time element, that Hull Rainer was close to his destination. If the route he had taken could be established, the rest would not be too difficult.

This area, Jason figured from what he had seen, was given over to small farms and the weekend cottages so beloved of Londoners. Most of the latter would not be used at this time of year. It was a sound possibility that Hull Rainer was keeping his wife locked in a house he had commandeered—perhaps one owned by someone he knew to be abroad, someone in the acting profession.

The more Jason thought of this, the better he liked it. He was encouraged by the fact of him having guessed right about Rainer's planted car. He decided that when the search began he would ignore farms and concentrate on the weekend cottages.

———————◆———————

"How do I know it's true?" David Reece asked.
Hull frowned as if puzzled. "If what's true?"
"That you could only get fifty thousand quid."

"I can't see why you'd want to doubt me, Dave."

"No?"

"Look. If we can't trust each other in this deal, there's certainly no one else we can trust. I'm being straight with you, Dave. I could only raise fifty grand."

The ex-burglar sniffed. He reached behind him to the mantel and got his bottle of beer. After drinking from the neck, he belched and said, "Okay, Hull boy. I believe you."

"Thanks," Hull said, ruffling himself as though hurt.

"Bring it with you?"

"What? Oh no, of course not. I need it in case the police do stick their noses in. They might demand to see it, treat it with chemicals."

"Right. So you make a phony drop tonight and then bring the money here with you tomorrow."

"Half of it," Hull said. "Half of it, Dave."

"Sure. Natch." Reece came and sat at the table. "Then we let her go, and it's all over."

Hull made rings on the table with his beer glass. "Be better all round if we held on to her for a while. Three or four days."

"No, thanks."

"Couple of days more wouldn't matter, Dave."

Reece said, "Mate, you do anything you want with Elsie after tomorrow. Hide her for a month if you like. When you take her from here she's all yours."

Hull straightened his spine. "*I* take her?"

The host raised his eyebrows. "What's wrong with that?"

"Look. It was agreed that Elsie was *your* job. You'd snatch her, you'd keep her, you'd take her away to be found."

While looking at the ceiling, Reece ran a thoughtful tongue forward and back over one of his broken teeth. The man's evil, Hull thought. Rotten to the core. No soul at all. Rob his own mother.

"Seems to me," David Reece said, looking down, "that I'm the boy that's doing all the risky stuff. Two thirds of it's already done, or near enough. Might be an idea if you did the last third yourself."

"That," Hull said, showing a firmness he didn't feel, "is what you're being paid for—to do the Elsie side of it. I'm the organiser. I set it up."

"Fine. Be the brain. Go ahead. Suits me. But you're wrong about my pay. It's not only for supplying transport, and board and lodging, and guard duty. It's for keeping my mouth shut."

Hull rose to get away from the mocking, clever eyes which, at close range, appeared to be looking deep inside him. He went to the hearth and stood with his back to the fire.

What Hull wanted to do was order David Reece to stick to the original agreement. He couldn't. But after a moment he did find a face-saver for giving in. He said:

"As a matter of fact, Dave, I was thinking of doing it myself anyway. Since hearing the law was onto a grey van, I decided using it again would be dangerous."

Reece looked disgruntled. With brattish sulkiness he said, "There's thousands of vans like mine. That don't mean nothing. I could do it easy. I'm just not going to, that's all. Not unless, well, unless I get paid extra for it."

"No no, Dave," Hull said brightly, teetering on his toes. "You were quite right. I should do it myself. And I will."

The ex-burglar slapped the beer bottle to his mouth and upended it.

Hull said, "Well, if you're sure you don't want to go into the village today, I see no sense in me staying here. I have things to do." He took a piece of paper from his pocket and put it on the table. "That's the London number I want you to call at eight o'clock on the dot."

Reece thudded the bottle down. "You want what?"

Hull airily explained about the police tap on the telephone in the Berkeley Square booth. He ended, "So I can't pretend to receive a call, you see. Call me there at eight sharp, please."

"What if I don't, or can't?"

"Then, that would mean the kidnapper had failed to make contact, which would mean I couldn't give him the ransom, which means I couldn't bring your share here tomorrow."

David Reece grunted and looked away. Hull said, "And

don't call from here, of course. They might have some new miracle gadget for tracing brief calls."

"What am I supposed to say?"

Hull told him. "Then ring off. Okay?"

"Yeah."

Breezy, Hull said, "Fine. You have your orders. Now I'll be off. Sure you're not going out?"

Reece pursed his fat lips, shook his head and said, "I've had enough excitement for one day." He smiled. "That Elsie."

Hull stiffened. "What about her?"

"Nothing, Hull boy. Nothing at all. Off you go."

After a short hesitation, another question flopping in his mouth, Hull turned sharply to the door and went out. He assured himself that he'd won. He had put the snotty bastard in his place. That crack about Elsie—a childish and lying try at attack. And the fool had swallowed the fifty-grand story.

But Hull's triumph congealed as he got in the Ford. So what?—he thought. He drove away dejectedly.

Five minutes later, slowing at the crossroads, he toyed with the idea of going in The Jolly Miller and cheering himself with a drink. He decided not. Ever since leaving home his thoughts had returned constantly to the case of money in his bedroom. What if the place were burglarised?

And now Hull got a more terrifying thought: What if David Reece had arranged for a colleague to break in?

Hull left the junction behind quickly.

Without incident he parked the Ford in its lot, shed his appearance-changers while walking to an Underground station, got the MGB and drove home. He ran up the back stairs and hustled inside the apartment and ran into his bedroom.

The money was safe. Hull had to lie down until his tension eased. Afterwards, he put the attaché case underneath soiled linen in the bathroom laundry basket.

Until four o'clock, Hull paced the apartment fretfully. He worried about his phony delivery of the money, about Elsie and the soul-less Reece, about getting his wife safely off his hands in town tomorrow.

In respect of the last, he thought the best way would be to give her a sleeping draft, lay her in the back of the Ford under a blanket, and look for some quiet spot in a suburb to put her out.

Hull took a tranquilizer and sat down to wait for Andrew Wilson of *Time*. He wanted to be composed, to photograph well.

Four o'clock came and went. At half past, Hull concluded he had been let down again. At five, he was irked enough to do something about it. He went to the directory to find the number of *Time*'s London offices.

The telephone rang. Hull answered. It was a friend asking for news. Mechanically, Hull said the things he always said. On disconnecting he tossed the directory aside. He had lost interest. He told himself that in any case, with Elsie being released tomorrow, the story would be over and Time wouldn't use the pictures.

He went to his room to siesta. His brain was too active. It kept him from sleep with scenes of all his worries coming to technicolour fruition. An hour of this and he got up.

After a snack, prepared and eaten slowly to fill time, and then a leisurely bath, Hull changed into a dark suit and a black shirt. He added a white tie, a dark slouch hat. The outfit looked suitably gangsterish, sinister. It perked his spirits, in spite of the fact that he was performing only for himself. He spent some minutes posing in front of a full-length mirror with the lights dimmed.

From a storage closet off the kitchen he got a stack of newspapers. He folded and wrapped and loosely tied them until he had formed a package approximating the size he wanted. Should the police interfere with the pre-drop and demand to examine the money—and he failed to see why they should—he would say he was going to try and fool the kidnappers.

At seven-thirty he went down to the basement, got in his car, drove it up and parked by the entrance of the apartment house. It was fully dark now. The street seemed to be deserted. But Hull felt sure that Wilkinson's men would be around somewhere. He went inside and back upstairs.

Fifteen minutes later he came down again. He was carrying the package and holding it with the reverence due its supposed contents. In the car he set the block of newsprint on the passenger seat. He drove off.

Marble Arch, Park Lane, Mount Street, Berkeley Square. In constant traffic Hull drove twice around the oblong looking for a spot to park. There were none. He double-parked near the telephone box. His watch gave the time as five minutes of eight.

He got out of the MGB and lit a cigarette. His hands were unsteady. He thought it was clever of him to do this in order to show police observers how nervous he was.

As he was moving toward the booth, its telephone rang. Hull flicked away his cigarette and went into the box. He lifted the receiver: "Hello. Rainer here."

The voice of David Reece, muffled, said, "Code XYZ. Go to Soho and drive around. You'll be contacted." The line clicked.

Hull dropped the receiver into its cradle and hustled out of the booth. He got in his car and drove off. In three minutes he was entering the narrow streets of Soho. Heavy traffic he had left behind him. Here cars were mostly parked. But there were still some in motion, at the back and ahead.

Hull twisted and turned along dim streets. His eyes darted in every direction. He was in a hurry to find the ideal place.

He passed an alley mouth, stopped, reversed, drove into the alley and along it at speed. There was no car behind. Spaced at the sides were piles of junk awaiting garbage collection, much of it wastepaper from stores.

By one such pile Hull squealed to a stop. He picked up the parcel, quickly ripped it apart, flung it out of the window, drove on. There was still no one behind.

Hull turned onto a street, swung around the first corner he came to, pulled into the side and stopped. He got out. He stood there as if bewildered.

There was a short wait before a taxi came to a gradual halt

thirty feet away. He could hear its radio squawking. The two passengers made no move to get out. Hull looked the other way. A man and a woman were strolling along, weaving as if tipsy. They and the pair in the taxi, Hull felt sure, were police.

He ignored them, made the gesture of flapping his arms against his sides as if in finality and resignation, got back in the car and drove on. He went slowly. The taxi kept behind at a distance. It closed in only when Hull had reached the block of flats in Lancaster Gate. He stopped at the kerb. The cab drew up behind.

As Hull alighted, a man was coming from the taxi. It was bald and grave Detective-Sergeant Bart. He looked around when a black car came to a fast halt behind the cab, went back and opened its door. He came forward again with Chief Inspector Harold Wilkinson.

Hull began talking before the men reached him. "It all happened so fast. One second he was there, the next gone. Did you get a chance to see him? I hope he didn't see *you*. If anything happens to Elsie—"

"Take it easy," Wilkinson said. He gave three ponderous puffs on his pipe, as if signalling for peace. "We saw no one and no one saw us. Now, Mr. Rainer, perhaps you could tell us what happened."

Hull took a deep breath. "Yes. Okay. But there's not much to tell. I drove around for a few minutes and then a man stepped into the road. He flagged me down, came to the window and said, 'XYZ. Give me the money.' I did. I asked about Elsie. He said she'd be there in Soho tomorrow night."

"What did he look like, sir?"

"His face was in shadow. I couldn't see a thing. Obviously he'd chosen the place with care. He wore a blue boilersuit and rubber boots, just like the other man. But this one was better and not so heavy. But I did get the impression there was someone else in a doorway."

Still talking, Hull got out cigarettes. He was calming. He knew he had pulled it off.

Like a thief, Jason crept in darkness toward the cottage. The night was as black as an enemy's sin. To see his way, Jason played on the ground an occasional beam from the flashlight he had bought in a country store. While there he had also, on an inspiration, asked if a stranger had been in buying provisions lately—explaining that he was a salesman looking for new residents. The owner had seen no one new since summer had ended.

The cottage was silent and its windows were dark. But that didn't necessarily mean desertion, Jason knew. The occupiers could have retired early, and if Elsie was here, alone, she would be quiet.

During the afternoon and evening, since getting that zigzag thrill on seeing Hull Rainer come to the crossroads from the left, Jason had visited more than thirty country retreats. Almost without exception they were cute-e-fied to look like country retreats. They owned crazy paving, cart wheels leaned casually on rough-finish walls, imitation shutters, flowerpots painted in bright colours, swinging lanterns and logs branded with the inevitable cozy name.

Two thirds of these places had been occupied. Jason had asked for his friend Carson with the green Ford who lived somewhere in the area. He had also been watchful for signs of nervousness in the occupiers. But that was a side idea. He felt sure Rainer was in this alone.

At the dozen cottages whose gates and doors were padlocked, Jason had tapped and called out at every window, as well as investigating outhouses. Leaving each property, there had always been the terrible feeling that Elsie was there, inside, bound and gagged and unable to answer his call. Knowing she couldn't be at every place made no difference. He always had that feeling, a heaviness in his stomach.

He had it now when, after tapping on a curtained window, he heard nothing but the moan of the wind. He wanted to break in, smash the glass. Which, he soothed himself, would be insane and pointless—unless he came across a definite indication, in which case he would be entitled to break fifty windows.

Jason went on. He arrived back where he had started, at the door. He knocked. The sound skittered away into the darkness. Jason shivered. He was cold. His hands and feet were as void of feeling as if they were not members at all but inadmissible objects.

He knocked again on the wood whose grain had been created with paint. In trying to peer through the letter slot he dropped his flashlight. He picked it up wearily.

He was not, Jason realised, operating at peak efficiency. This didn't surprise him when, on looking at his wristwatch, he saw that it was nine o'clock. He had been on the move solidly for seven hours, which had been preceded by more hours of tense waiting.

The cottage remaining silent, Jason turned away with that heavy pull in his stomach. He had approached on sound-deadening grass; he left crunchily on the seashell path.

Tomorrow was another day, he told himself. In the morning he would be rested and alert. Now he needed a warming drink and something to eat.

He came out onto the narrow road. His motorcycle was leaned against the hedge. Wondering if he should try one more place before calling it quits for the night, Jason played the beam of his flashlight over the next gate along, and then the one across the way.

Both gates were of farms, which he knew by their plain and strong build, even without their names—Martin's Poultry Ltd, and Apple Acres.

So quits it was, Jason thought. He got on his motorcycle and shattered the night's peace with the engine.

Three miles back he came to the junction and The Jolly Miller. He parked outside the pub, went in. There were twenty-odd customers, all countryfolk with sturdy clothes and ruddy complexions. The landlord was the man who had served earlier.

Jason ordered a double whisky with hot water and lemon, asked about food, learned he could have a sandwich or ham and veal pie. He settled on the latter, with pickled onions.

The words made him realise his hunger. Also, they made him feel guilty. Was Elsie being fed properly?—he wondered. Was she on bread and water? Was she on anything at all?

He put the questions aside. They would lead inevitably to the big one he had so far avoided: whether or not Elsie was alive. As for his own food, he told himself he had to keep up his strength for the search.

After serving pie and drink, the landlord asked, "Did you get to find your friend, sir?"

"Ah yes," Jason said. "Yes, I did, thank you. He lives miles away. I—um—came back on this same route because I noticed what a lot of cottages there are. The south road, I mean."

A huge farmer beside Jason at the bar said, "City people mostly." He shook his head. The landlord, a diplomat, added that they were all right so long as they didn't try to drink cider and kept their dogs under control.

Jason asked, "How many places would you say there were on that ten-mile stretch of road?"

Landlord and farmer sucked in their breath noisily. It was not encouraging. After a short debate the men agreed on the number of noncommercial properties as two hundred. Jason said he had a vague idea of buying something for weekends.

"I wonder if you know which are empty, up for sale?" he asked.

Again the two men debated, reaching no agreement. Both scribbled on bits of paper, which they gave to Jason. The landlord's list was of cottages for sale or rent ("Them's the only ones I've heard about"). The farmer's list was of people to contact ("Those three get around a bit and they know everything").

Jason asked the men to have a drink with him. They accepted. Over the following half hour, while nibbling at the pie, which was so tasty that guilt made him leave half of it,

Jason managed to steer the talk to cottage-owning actors, to MGBs and green Fords, to that kidnapping case that had been in the papers: "Vanetti, was it, and Hull Rainer?" Although he learned nothing, he felt confident. He was sure that sometime tomorrow he would find what he was looking for.

This was in his mind as he drove back to London. Specifically, the risk of unseen dangers in the act of finding. It was possible that Hull Rainer was not alone in this, Jason thought. There was the chance of him actually being innocent, forced to play along, the lever in some form of extortion.

When near home, Jason changed course and went to the suburb where he worked.

He propped his motorcycle and let himself into the office. Putting a match to the gas fire, he crouched over it until suppleness had returned to his hands. He turned the fire off and sat at the desk.

After rolling a carbon sandwich into the typewriter, he got out that indispensible street guide, *London A to Z*, in order to have place names right—the church, the department store, the movie house.

He started typing. For ten minutes he worked, most of that time spent in thought as he strove for brevity. Finished, he read the page through:

*I, Jason Galt, suspecting Hull Rainer of being implicated in the kidnapping of his wife, followed him today, September 14, when he left home at midday in his MGB. He drove to St. James's Anglican church on Argyle Street, parked and walked to Hartfield Parade, where he entered Woolworth's and left again by a back door. While going along the alley he put on a scarf, glasses and a cap to alter his appearance. He got in a taxi, number OTG 7242, from the rank on William Penn Avenue and went to Drummond Road. From there he walked to the car park behind the Odeon cinema on the same street, where he got in a green Ford, number XLN 3748, and drove into Berkshire. Beyond Compton Pool he turned south at The*

*Jolly Miller crossroads, where I lost contact. I intend
going back there tomorrow morning to search empty
houses, in one of which, I am convinced, I will find Elsie
Vanetti.*

The top copy Jason placed in an envelope, which he
addressed To Whom It May Concern before putting it carefully inside his windcheater. The carbon copy he folded and
slipped into a pocket of his jeans. He locked up the office and
went out.

Driving away through the pub- and cinema-leaving traffic,
Jason felt good about what he thought of as the letter of in-
surance. The gambit was as old as crime fiction, but it often
worked. And if it didn't work in this case, as rescue, it would
as posthumous revenge.

At Shank Place he struggled his motorcycle up the front
steps and left it in the hall. Upstairs, he propped the envelope
in a prominent position on the living-room table, went into the
kitchen and fixed himself hot chocolate as an aid to sleeping.

It wasn't needed. Five minutes after dropping fully dressed
on the bed he was in a deep sleep.

Jason awoke the next morning at eight. By a quarter of nine
he was eating breakfast in Compton Pool's only café, by a
quarter after was making his first call.

The place had looked empty from the road. Now, as Jason
approached the front door, it burst open and a young couple
came chasing out, the girl first. She wore a robe; he was in pa-
jama bottoms. They came to an awkward halt and gaped at
the newcomer with undefinable expressions. Both began to
blush. The situation said Illicit Love Nest. As embarrassed as
they were, Jason mumbled a covering story and left.

The next cottage was empty. Even better, the windows
were uncurtained. It took him five minutes to check the place
out. He climbed a low wall which divided properties and
went to the neighbour, a wooden structure in Swiss-chalet
style. Front and back doors had cobwebs which had been
there a long time. He went back to the road.

An hour Later, Jason was still looking. He was not disheartened. Every wrong place he called at brought the right place closer.

———————◆———————

The man in the stocking mask was straddling the chair. Like a tennis spectator in slow motion, his head followed Elsie as she paced back and forth across the room.

It wasn't nerves that kept Elsie moving. Yesterday's exertions and the bruises gained in her attempt to escape had left her body with an all-over ache. This increased when she walked. The mild suffering was almost as good as having something to do.

She paced with head down, which hid the walls from her view, and with her arms folded tight and high, which prevented her breasts from swaying.

Elsie had been through all the classic emotions of captivity. She no longer knew if she liked or loathed the perpetual day of the naked bulb above, the bed which was a refuge of sleep and a constant reminder of her shame, the little fire that was ugly and a comfort.

There were times when she felt like laughing with joy at being alive, others when she had to use all her will power to hold back from clawing the door.

It was the same in relation to the man. She hated him, and she hated herself for being relieved whenever he came in. It sickened her that she looked forward to his visits and dreaded their end.

Elsie started now and stopped pacing as he got up from the chair. He stretched. He said, "Well, must get back to work."

"No," Elsie said. She hugged herself with folded arms. "Let's talk awhile."

"Oh, I dunno. I'm still angry with you, y'know."

"Why? Sit down. Please."

He shrugged, sat. "Yesterday. You were very bad. You could've got me into real big trouble with the other boys."

"Sorry. I didn't mean it."

"Don't be silly. Course you did."

"No," Elsie said. She went to stand opposite her guard to lend force to her words. "I didn't plan it. Trying to escape without my clothes on—that couldn't have been planned. It was on the spur of the moment."

"You mean you were going to go through with the bargain?"

Elsie looked down. Her lie had backfired. She said, "I was trying to. I don't know."

"Well, dearie, whatever it was, you spoiled things for yourself. You missed out on a lot of extra comforts."

"I don't care."

"You don't?"

"It's this room," Elsie said. "It's getting me down. It seems to get smaller every—" She broke off as her voice began to rise.

The man put his head on one side. "Not interested any more in books, hot water, a radio and them other things? That's too bad. It's lovely little radio. All kinds of programmes."

"Don't. You aren't helping. You're being cruel."

"Me? I'm as kind as the day's long."

Elsie went to the bed and sat. "There's nothing I want."

The man said in a low tone. "Oh yes, there is."

"What?"

"You want to get out."

"Of course." She spoke dully. She sank to a huddle over her folded arms.

Slow and low the man said, "That, dearie, might be arranged."

Indifferently: "I don't believe you."

"Why not?"

"Because I don't."

"A deal's a deal, remember. I wouldn't let you down."

Elsie mumbled in tired derision. The man asked, "Did I let you down with the books? Did I let you down with the comb?"

"Well, no."

"There you are, then."

Elsie came up slightly out of her huddle and looked at the man. He was sitting forward on the chair. After a moment's silence she said, "Go on."

He said, "Don't know as I should tell you. You don't seem interested."

"I am. I'm listening."

The man rubbed the side of his face, stretching the stocking mask weirdly. "Well, it's like this, see. I'm not really in on this deal. They paid me to get you and bring you here and to fetch you your meals. What they're up to I don't know. That's why I told you not to ask me any questions. Remember? It's cos I don't know any answers."

Elsie was losing her disinterest and disbelief. She said, "Please go on."

"Me, I'm just a worker. I was broke and needed the money. I'll be every bit as glad as you are when it's all over. And that'll be today. For me. My job finishes this evening."

Elsie sat straight. "What's going to happen?"

"They're taking you to a different place," the man said. "It's not as good as this. You won't be well-treated there. Me, I'm not a bad bloke. Them others, they're a tough bunch. They hate you, seems to me."

"Hate me?"

He lifted his shoulders. "Don't ask me why. I don't get it either. I think, though, that it's something to do with the acting game. Maybe they're jealous cos you're real big. There's women in this too." He paused, shook his head. "I'm telling you too much."

"No," Elsie said earnestly. She felt like going to him and giving him pats and tugs of encouragement. "Please go on."

"Well," the man said, "that's really all I know, or can guess. What I do know is that things aren't going to be so easy for you from now on. Not a nice bunch, them lot. They've even been rotten to me. You'd think I was a bloody lackey or something."

It was possible, Elsie thought, that the man was in the

mood for rebellion because of bad treatment. She asked, 'How many of these people are there?"

He shook his head again. "No more info."

"All right. Fine. Frankly, I don't care. But you said you could arrange for my escape."

"*Might*, I said. That depends on you."

"I'm listening."

"The thing is," the man said, his tone confidential, "they'll all be away this afternoon for a while. I'll be on me own here. So, if I felt like it, what I could do is put you in a car and drive you into another district and let you out. Then I'd clear off myself. I've already been paid."

"I see. Yes, I see." She was trying not to hope, to believe fully. A disappointment would be too hard to take.

The man said, "But I'd have to be paid by you as well."

Elsie stood up. All hope and belief, she said quickly, "I'll give you ten thousand pounds."

"Sit down," the man said, waving a descending hand. "Go on, sit down."

She sat, asking, "How much? Are you going to tell me how much you want?"

"Yes, and it's not money. If you had it here—fine. I'd take it like a shot. But you got no money here, and I couldn't count on getting it later, afterwards. Even if you wanted to pay up, the law wouldn't let you."

"They couldn't stop me."

"Or they might let you go through with it and then grab me. No, dearie, money's out. There's only one way."

Elsie said, "Oh."

"I'll tell you my terms and then I'll leave you for an hour to make up your mind. All right?"

She nodded. "All right."

"What we'd do is this. You get undressed and into bed. For safety's sake I'd tie your right hand up on the post. I'd put the light out. We'd be nice and cozy."

Elsie asked, "For fifteen minutes?"

The man waved his hand sideways. "Oh no, dearie. That

was yesterday's deal, in exchange for a few comforts. This is for something big. You don't realise what a chance I'm taking. These are tough people, I tell you."

"How long?"

"Two hours."

She had nothing to say. The man went on, "And that's not all. You'd have to act like you meant it. You'd have to be real keen. None of that cold stuff. Understand me?"

Elsie nodded. The man got up and went toward the door. "So that's the deal. Think it over. In exchange you get your freedom. I'll be back." He went out and locked the door behind him.

Elsie, returning to her huddle, stared wretchedly at the floor.

———————————◄◆►——————————

The sun was high, the sky clear. The morning had a smell of freshness like a mountaintop and there was a tactile bite of frost in the air. A glimmer of hoar coated the flora, which as yet had not been touched by the sun.

The field Jason was striding across had the hardness of planking. He felt like that himself: tough, unresistant, implacable. He would allow no hindrance in his search. He even had a secret longing for someone to oppose him so that he could have something to hit.

The morning had not been without incident in that respect. Already in his routine of crossing land between close-set properties instead of going back to the road and cycling to the next lane, he had been attacked by a dog, which he had kicked into yipping retreat; for trampling a smidgin of crop had been snarled at by a farmer, whom he had outsnarled and ultimately cowed; been railed at nervously by a startled, washing-hanging woman, who fast calmed at his apologetic and self-assured manner, and even gave him the names of six local friends he needn't bother to call on because they were in residence and their homes were not on the market.

At one point, the blood hammering in his temples, Jason

had thought his search was finally over. He had heard a voice. High in pitch, it had been calling for help.

He had broken into a run on the narrow path of gravel between tall, mazelike hedges. Coming out into the open he had found three teen-agers. The two boys were chasing the girl, owner of the voice. They didn't see him. Unsteadily he had crept away.

Now, crossing the field, Jason reckoned that soon he would be halfway through the possible hiding places. Every call, he felt, brought him closer to Elsie.

And this one might well be it, he thought.

The cottage was built of wood and painted white with red trim. The curtains were drawn across the windows, a good sign. A better sign was that no smoke curled from the chimney, which, because of its soot stains, was obviously a real one and not the cute piece of decoration which topped so many of the country retreats.

Jason stepped over a strand of saggy barbed wire and went the last twenty yards to the door. He knocked.

At first there was nothing, except the echo of his knock bouncing back from a nearby garage. Then from inside sounded a shuffling. It came right to the door, which opened six inches to reveal a woman. She wore a chenille robe and had on a scarf to hide rollers. Her age was in the thirty-to-forty range.

"Good morning," Jason said. He ran both hands over his hair: helmet and goggles had been left at the motorcycle.

The woman said, "Hello."

"I hope I didn't disturb you."

She smiled. "No, that's all right. I was just getting up. Lazy me. Was there something?"

Jason gave the story he had been using as an alternative, a change of pace. "Well, ma'am, I was talking to a man yesterday back at The Jolly Miller, didn't catch his name, but he told me he lives on this road. His car's for sale, you see. I'm interested."

"What's he look like?"

Jason described Hull Rainer in his semi-disguise, adding, "The car's a two-year-old Ford. Green."

The woman was shaking her head. "Can't say he sounds familiar."

From behind her came a thumping sound. Jason tensed. He recalled last night's idea, one of those which had made him write the letter: Rainer might not be alone in the kidnapping: Elsie could have a guard. And wasn't this woman a little too pleasant, too much the allayer of suspicion?

The thumping sounded again.

Blandly Jason asked, "Who are you hiding back there?"

The woman gave a series of blinks. "What?" Next she laughed. "Oh, that. It's my sister. She's like me, loves a lie-in on a cold morning. Who doesn't?"

"Sounds as if she's locked herself in."

The woman nodded as if absently. "A cap and glasses and around thirty. Now let me think."

So?—Jason mused, still tense. What's the next move? Push inside and see who's making the noise? Knock the woman down if she gets in the way? If Elsie's back there, great. If she isn't . . .

It occurred to Jason for the first time that in cases like this he could use hypnotism. He could put the householder into a trance, make a quick search, disentrance the person and leave him ignorant of what had happened.

From inside the house sounded footsteps. They were approaching. The woman glanced back and pushed the door wide. Behind her appeared another woman, of similar age and similar state of undress, who smiled in similar fashion—one who, it now seemed to Jason, was being coquettish rather than merely friendly.

The newcomer said, "Gin makes me sleep late. Good morning. Are you a salesman?"

"No, ma'am."

"I've heard all about salesmen."

"Don't be naughty," her sister said. "He's looking for someone." She explained.

The other woman shrugged. "Not familiar. But nothing is till I've had my tea." She smiled at Jason. "Like to come in and have a cup?"

That, the invitation, was good enough absolution as far as Jason was concerned. He said, "Thanks all the same. I don't have the time. Maybe later." He turned smartly and left.

On the way back to the road, he thought again of Elsie having a guard, or guards, which reminded him of all the places he had passed by, dismissed as being unlikely prospects. He realised he had been wrong to rule out farms. Elsie could be anywhere.

Jason was taken by a sense of urgency. He began to run.

———◆———

The hour was nearly up. Elsie had not yet decided. Her mind was so busy she was hardly aware of her pacing and circling, her stops to press on the door and walls, her sudden and brief bouts of shivering.

She was still weighing the pros and cons. They had been repeating themselves drearily/hopefully ever since the man had left her to make up her mind. These were interspersed with scenes of magic. Elsie saw herself doing wonderful, improbable things.

She saw herself eating toast from which the butter oozed and dribbled. She saw herself strolling along a street with Jason Galt. She saw herself switching on a television set and then airily switching it off again. She saw herself looking at the sky, examining a leaf, breathing the evening air. She saw herself turning on a tap and watching the hot, steaming water go gurgling away down the drain. She saw herself changing into fresh, sweet-smelling clothes.

And then, after each magical scene, it was back to the pros and cons of payment.

Could she stand it? Would she feel so degraded that she'd cry, scream, start to fight? If so, the whole thing would come to nothing. And if she stood it for the first while and then revolted later, the sacrifice of that first while would be wasted, she would have suffered it for nothing—the man would call the deal off.

And could she, most difficult of all, pretend to respond? Would she, unable to stop herself, recoil from his touch? or snarl at him to leave her alone? or out of revulsion deny whatever innovation he might demand?

And if he at the end of that two-hour eternity was satisfied, would he keep to the bargain? What if he—such a cruel sense of humour he had—if he simply laughed and said more fool you for believing me?

Elsie paced, touched the walls, ran her hands over the door, fought back tears.

And a return to the scenes of magic. She saw herself lying in her wide, soft bed. She saw herself soaking in a hot bath and washing her hair with suds like cream. She saw herself stroking the clothes in her wide closet and being unable to decide on which garment to wear. She saw herself sitting on the grass in Hyde Park and listening to children's laughter.

Elsie clenched her fists. She thought again of the pros. They were good and solid, not created out of despair.

There was the fact that Jason had said, apropos of a play they had seen, that prostitution was honourable, a matter of supply and demand, a straightforward exchange of cash for a service in which the buyer got exactly what he paid for with no cheating or false claims; a business more honest than ninety per cent of advertisements and much of the world's other commerce.

There was the point she had read, and accepted, that a kiss on the mouth was far more intimate, personal, and connecting to the inner self than the act of sexual congress.

There was the fact that the light would be off. In the darkness the man could be anyone. She could forget she hated him, that he had tortured her and was abusing her. She could use her imagination. She could pretend he was her husband.

Elsie shook her head. She didn't care for that, because she had a husband and he was Hull. She thought, I could pretend he was Jason.

Ridiculously, she felt herself blushing. She hurried her musing.

There was the fact that she was an actress. She could put on a convincing performance. Friends had told her of times when, despite illness or unhappiness, she had walked onstage and carried off her role with skill. She could act the part of the man's loving wife, or a Mata Hari seductress, or a harlot happy to be earning a large fee. She could put on a marvellous, award-winning performance.

Elsie felt sick, dizzy, exhausted. Going to the bed of hateful possibilities, she let herself fall onto it face down and began to sob tiredly.

———◆———

Jason steered his motorcycle through the open gateway. His face and body were tense. This was the second call of his new urgency, the feeling of time running out which caused him, as on the first call, not to leave his machine on the road but take it right up to the property—regardless of the fact that this could give warning of approach to anybody with something—or someone—to hide.

But, as he bounced along the rough track, he did keep the engine low, humming, letting impetus carry him toward the buildings.

The place didn't look promising. Although not quite a farm, which its name on the gate had implied, neither was it like the other weekend retreats Jason had seen. It lacked the size and the equipment of the first, the tidy prettiness of the second. It was merely a jumble of brick sheds.

Jason, however, had made up his mind to stick to the resolution that everything should be checked out, even if it were a mansion.

The track was slightly downhill. Jason switched off the engine and coasted in neutral. Now there was only the squeal of leather and the whine of springs.

He reached the buildings, went between two of them and was in the yard, eased to a stop beside a muddy vehicle, sat with a leg supporting him at either side. He looked around.

The place seemed deserted, which made it a good prospect in relation to Jason's initial ideas on how Elsie would be held prisoner. Though what didn't fit was the gate standing open.

One of the buildings looked like the house, despite the absence of curtains at the windows, the glass of which was streaked with dirt and cracked in several places. The paintwork was pale with age. The neglect showed everywhere.

Jason got quietly off the motorcycle. He propped it, stood back, turned—and started with surprise. He was being watched. The man seemed to have appeared out of the air.

Body prickle over, Jason took one step forward. "Well, hello," he said. "Good morning."

The man nodded. He was standing some twenty feet away by the corner of the next building, leaning there. His face expressed neither interest, friendliness nor antagonism. The inscrutability reminded Jason of Chief Inspector Wilkinson.

Uncertain of himself and his line of approach, though feeling hopeful, Jason took another step forward. He asked, "I wonder if you could help me, please."

The man nodded again. "Maybe," he said.

"The thing is, I'm looking for someone."

"What's the name?"

"*My* name?"

The man shook his head. "The one what you're looking for."

"I don't know it."

He pushed himself upright from his lean on the corner, saying mildly, "You don't know who you're looking for, eh?"

Jason explained about the green Ford supposedly for sale and its name-unknown owner. He watched the bland face closely for reactions when he ended:

"He's in his thirties, has glasses, wears a cap and a scarf."

There was no appreciable response. The man raised a hand and with a dirty fingernail scratched the point of his chin, not as if in answer to an itch but to help in thought.

"You can tell he's not used to glasses," Jason said. "So perhaps he only got them recently."

The man said, "Don't b'lieve I know him."

"He looks as if he might be an actor. He's got that way with him."

The man went on scratching. "No. He don't sound like anyone I know."

Jason made another stab close to the heart: "He's only in these parts during the early afternoon."

"No," the man said. He stopped scratching his chin and with forefinger and thumb stroked downwards on his long, grey-black moustache. He was middle-aged and wore a corduroy suit spattered with mud.

Jason was about to move forward, hope growing, when again he was startled: the man turned his head and shouted. He called out a name.

The door of the building opposite, the one which looked like the house, opened with a speed that could only mean the opener had been waiting, holding the handle. A younger man came out and moved partway toward the other. He was in slovenly overalls.

Following him from the house came a youth. Next appeared three children and a teen-age girl. Last, another child and a woman moved to stand framed in the doorway. It was as if the man's shout had been a signal that the coast was clear.

Although his hope had gone, Jason was amused by the parade. He withstood the stares and waited patiently while his visit was explained by the first man, who prefaced it with:

"I reckon this fella's all right. He ain't a copper and he ain't a gamekeeper."

There was a discussion in which everyone joined, including the youngest child. No one knew the owner of the green Ford.

The younger man asked, "You wouldn't be interested in a couple of nice pheasants, would you, sir?"

"No," Jason said. "No, thanks. And thank you for trying to help. Good morning."

He turned to leave. Then he turned back on remembering another angle. He pulled pieces of paper from the hip pocket of his jeans. A small piece he kept, putting the others back.

"I've got three names here," he said. "They're people who

might be able to give me a lead. Perhaps you could tell me where they live."

The first man nodded. "Glad to. Who are they?"

Jason looked at the list given him by the farmer in The Jolly Miller. He read out, "Mrs. Sentine, Joss Whiteside, and David Reece."

---

The key scraped in the lock.

It was a terrible sound to Elsie. She jerked up to arm's length from her sprawl on the bed, where she had been lying in a near-catatonic state of dreariness. Her eyes, dry, changed from dead to quick.

The time was up and she still had reached no decision. Her inner debate on the question had ground to a halt, battered by repetition into the defeat of a punchy who can't give up but won't fall.

The door opened. In came the man, who no longer looked strange. The fawn patch of lumps and twists between hat and muffler seemed as natural as flesh and features. Elsie had felt lately that it would be improper of him to show his face.

She got off the bed. After taking two short, nervous steps away from it she stood with feet primly together, hands clasped at her waist, head slightly lowered.

The man locked the door and leaned on it casually. He slid the large key into his pocket, which he then gave a pat. He looked around the room.

"Cozy in here," he said. "You couldn't call it cold."

The lack of fresh air, Elsie's breathing and the constant electric fire had given the room a fogginess that was almost warmth. She said, "Yes."

"Not a bad little place at all."

"No."

"You couldn't say you've been ill-used, not really." His voice sounded strained.

Elsie wondered when he was going to get to the point. She wondered what she was going to say when he did.

"You've had your meals nice and regular. Hot, too. You didn't do badly here, did you?"

Elsie said, "The food was all right."

There followed a minute of silence. It was broken by the man clearing his throat. He said, "Well, now. Have you been thinking things over like a sensible girl?"

She felt like that, a girl, young and foolish and vulnerable. She felt she was making a mountain of trauma out of a molehill physical act which was as common as cleaning teeth or putting on shoes, which must be taking place a millionfold right this moment.

But she couldn't do it. She had decided. Whatever it was her body would buy, she couldn't go through with the performance.

Not waiting to be asked outright, Elsie said, "I'm sorry."

The man asked, "What's that?"

"I can't do it. Sorry. I can't make the deal with you."

He nodded slowly. "I don't want no nonsense, no haggling over times or anything. I want a final answer." His voice was no longer strained. It was firm and cold.

She said, "The answer is final. Definite."

"Sure you're not going to change your mind? It'll be too late later on."

"I'm sure."

The man pushed off the door and turned toward it. He gazed upward, as if not at the truncated view of beams but at a distance of sky. After a light sigh, he said:

"Pity. It's such a beautiful day out."

Elsie's whole body was taken by a tremor. She felt an ache inside her like the approach of tears. While looking at the floor she heard herself say, quickly and breathlessly, "Yes, all right."

"Eh?"

"All right. I'll do it."

"I didn't hear you," the man said. "What?"

She raised her whisper from low to loud. "I'll do it. The deal. What we talked about. You know." She had the terrible suspicion that he had been playing with her, that he had no intention of going through with it.

He asked, "What will we do exactly?"

She looked up. "You can't have forgotten. You can't have."

"No. But remind me. Go on."

"I'll get undressed," Elsie said. "I'll get into bed and you'll tie one hand, the right one, so I can't escape or try anything. There'll be no risk."

"And the light?"

"The light will be switched off so I can't see your face. You'll get undressed as well and we'll be together in the dark, nice and cozy as you wanted it."

The man asked, "For how long?"

"For two hours," Elsie said. "Two full hours."

"And how will *you* be?"

"Good. Very good. I'll do everything you want. You'll have nothing to complain about."

The man treated himself to that familiar knuckle-rub on the side of the face. "I'd be taking a hell of a chance, sneaking you away and letting you go."

Leaning forward earnestly, wringing her hands like a novel heroine, Elsie said, "For two long hours we'll be together and I promise you won't regret it and you'll be safe and I won't try to escape and all I'll do is give you whatever you want."

He grunted.

"Please," Elsie said. She said, "Please."

The man seemed to be looking at her, seemed to be considering. She stared back with worried eyes. The silence grew. At last the man cleared his throat and said, "Go on, dearie."

Eager, Elsie took off and tossed aside her cardigan. Crossing her arms she grasped the top hem and pulled the garment up and around her head, where it stopped.

In her haste she had forgotten to unfasten the small zipper at the back of the neck. She was caught there, helpless, arms and hair in a tangle, feeling the chill air.

"The zip," she gasped.

She heard the man coming closer, felt his hands on her back. She felt weird, nightmarish.

Dimly through the sweater she saw the man as he came around to the front. She watched him carefully and slowly lift the loosened girdle of cloth up over her breasts. She willed herself to be still.

Through the two curtains of material, hers and his, she could glimpse the twin specks of light of his eyes. She prayed for his pleasure.

"I can't breathe," she lied. "Quickly."

Still he took no notice. He stood back. His eyes gleamed, he had the stance of an ape.

Elsie kept still, watching the stocking mask's lower part where the mesh went in-out, in-out.

Straightening, he moved away and went around to the back. His fingers were unsteady as they fumbled with the zipper. He got it open. She pulled the garment off wearily and let it fall. Her face was damp with sweat.

Elsie moved to the bed. She got under the covers and lay on her back with one arm up behind her head.

She turned her face away, remembered her role and looked back again. The man, standing above her, said, "Smile."

She produced a trembly grimace. She held it while watching the man bring from his pocket a length of cord and, swiftly now, tie her right wrist to the iron bedpost.

He bent over her with his face close. He whispered, "You want me."

"I want you," she said, also speaking in a low tone. "Please get into bed with me quickly."

"You're going to earn every minute of your payment."

"I am. Every minute. I'm going to give you satisfaction."

"And you'll love it."

She whispered, "I'll love it. I'll enjoy all of it and make sure you enjoy it too."

"You're excited."

"I'm very excited. I can't wait."

"You're going—"

The man broke off. He stood suddenly upright. He turned his head. In a normal voice he said a sharp, "What was that?"

"What?"

"A noise. Sounded like a knock on the front door."

"No," Elsie said, keeping her tone at a whisper to encourage calm. "I didn't hear anything."

"I think it was a knock."

"It was nothing, nothing." Again she had the terrible dread that he was playing with her, or that something would happen to make him change his mind.

Body rigid, the man snapped, "I'm sure it was somebody at the door."

"No no. Please. Get undressed."

"Listen!" he hissed. "There it goes again. It's a knock. I'm sure it's a knock."

"It's nothing," Elsie pleaded. "The wind. Please get into bed with me."

"Shurrup," he said, turning away. "I'll be back in a minute."

"Don't go!" Elsie called. "For God's sake, don't go!"

Jason stood back from the house door. He was thinking it odd that his entering the yard noisily, as he had the other two places, had not roused the occupiers, who must be around because of the smoke from the chimney; yet there was a response of indoor movement now after his second knock. Odd that they hadn't heard the motorcycle.

Jason brushed it off. He told himself that the people could be in bed, like the sisters, or something equally innocuous, that he would have to stop finding strangeness in everyday quirks, it could lose him a lot of time.

From inside came a man's voice. It asked, "Who's there?"

Jason called, "Could I see you a minute, please?"

"What's it about?"

"Won't keep you long. I was given your name by someone."

After a pause the man asked, "Can you come back later?"

"Look. I'll only keep you a minute."

There was the sound of grumbling followed by a clear, "Hold on. I'll be out in a sec."

Turning, Jason looked around the yard. His motorcycle was propped against a shed. Nearby stood a small grey van. The place was scruffy and drear, despite the bright sun, which was up near its apex now.

The sun reminded Jason that he was warm. He took off the plastic raincoat and balled it up as he walked to his machine, where he stuffed it in the helmet strapped behind the saddle.

The house door opened. Jason walked back, seeing in the doorframe a man about forty years old. He wore a tweed jacket and riding britches. Of average build, he had a thick-lipped simian face and sharp eyes. He seemed, to Jason, to be agitated.

"Okay," he said shortly. "What's your problem?"

Jason gave a pleasant smile. "No problem. A man in The Jolly Miller gave me your name. He said you might be able to help me."

"Did he really. Well, well. What man?"

"A farmer. I don't know him."

"Then I don't know him either."

"You're Mr. Reece, aren't you? David Reece?"

Through his nose the man let out a sigh, one of exasperation, it seemed. "That's right."

"The farmer thought you could help me find someone."

"What am I supposed to be, mate, a missing-persons office?"

"Well—"

"Look. I'm busy. Real busy. I've got work in here."

Still smiling, Jason asked, "What kind of work?"

The man fluffed out his lips, stabbed fists to his waist. "It's none of your bloody business. Now, why don't you just piss off."

"You're not being very helpful, Mr. Reece."

"There's no reason in hell why I should be. *I* didn't give you my name. And I've told you I'm busy. I'm listening to the radio, to the foot-and-mouth precautions, and you've come right in the middle of it."

Could be so, Jason thought with descending hope. It would explain his anger and the fact that he hadn't heard the bike. Also a guilty man would try and allay suspicion with friendliness rather than arouse it by being obstructive.

"Now, if you'll kindly take yourself off, mate," David Reece said, "I can get back to my work."

"All right," Jason said. "Sorry. Maybe I'll call later, if you don't mind."

"This afternoon. Five or six."

"Okay. So long." Jason turned and walked to his motorcycle. He got on, kicked the engine alive and moved off. As he slowly circled the van he noted the windowless state of its body. That, he thought, would have made a perfect instrument for the abduction of Elsie from the block of flats.

Jason next wondered why, if the radio had been on in the house, he hadn't heard it himself. And, since there was no evidence of livestock, why the man was so keen on news of foot-and-mouth disease.

Suddenly, David Reece's aggression and agitation were all wrong. Hope on the rise again, Jason swung the motorcycle around.

The man saw him turn and went quickly from view, leaving the door open. By the time Jason had switched off his machine and dismounted, David Reece was back and coming determinedly outside. He was carrying a shotgun.

The gun gave further impetus to Jason's hope. He smiled broadly and felt his pulses quicken like a horse breaking from trot to gallop.

The man called Reece said, "Now look here, you." His face had grown dark with blood and ugly with belligerence.

"Hold it," Jason said cheerfully. "I'm going to tell you the real reason I came. I'll take a chance. I have to be careful, you know, but what the hell."

"Eh?"

The two men came to a halt. They were three feet apart. Jason said, "I've got something to sell. I think you might be interested. It's bent."

Reece obviously knew the slang term for stolen property, for he threw back, "I don't care how it is, mate. I'm not buying. Just piss off."

"A diamond," Jason said, bringing from his pocket a piece of jewellery. "A precious stone that's going for a song."

"Not interested," the man snapped, but he looked when the shiny, button-sized bauble was held up at eye level, dangling from its two inches of gilt chain.

Jason was rarely without his hypnotist's bauble. The reason was more than it being the main stock-in-trade of his profession. This item of dime-store jewellery had a special significance. He had used it with Elsie.

Moving his hand slightly he caused the trinket to move in a gentle and rhythmic pattern. Its shiny surface caught the sun and gave off jets of reflection. These flicked across Reece's face.

He grunted, "Looks like a piece of junk."

"It's supposed to," Jason said, his voice low and calm and slow. "That is the clever part. It is disguised. The diamond is worth twenty thousand pounds and it is hidden inside a piece of junk."

Reece frowned, staring. He appeared to be torn between aggression and curiosity. There was also a hint of greed in the purse of his lips.

"If you look closely at this piece," Jason said, "you will be able to see the truth. The beauty. The piece within the piece. Concentrate. See the wealth. A great piece of value, a piece of great value, a valuable piece."

Reece blinked slowly, his eyes on the moving trinket.

"Peace and calm," Jason crooned. "Peace and sleep. Peace and rest. Peace. Watch the peace and feel the calm. It can be yours. You can own it. You may possess the peace. You know how wonderful it would be to own peace, don't you? Don't you?"

David Reece's head gave a faint nod. His features had slackened. The tension had gone from his stance.

Jason asked with quiet insistence, "Don't you?"

The man murmured, "Yes." His tone had a childish meekness.

Jason went on talking softly and repetitively. At the same time he gradually reduced the movement of his hand. His voice purred to a stop to coincide with the cessation of the sway of the bauble.

David Reece had his mouth open. His eyelids were heavy. His body was slack. His face had no expression.

Jason whispered, "Close your eyes and find peace in sleep."

Reece lowered his eyelids while giving a deep sigh. He was entranced. Jason put away his bauble, ordering, "Drop the object you are holding." The shotgun fell to the ground. Reece stood on in motionless sleep.

Jason ran. He raced to the house and inside. There was a parlour, untidy, a fire burning in the grate. He listened as he looked around. There was not a sound to be heard. He called out, "Elsie?" Still no sound.

By the hearth was an open doorway. He went through it quickly into a kitchen. There was nothing out of the ordinary, and the tall closet he yanked open held only brushes.

Back again in the other room, Jason saw a stairway door. He crossed to it and went up in four long strides and kept on going into a bedroom. He was surprised to find it empty. He checked in the wardrobe and under the bed. Out on the landing he went into another bedroom. It was empty also, as was the bathroom.

With slightly less urgency, Jason descended the stairs. He was beginning to have doubts, thought he could have been wrong in his suspicions of David Reece. But he reminded himself that the search wasn't over yet.

Back in the parlour he noticed a third interior doorway. He strode to it and looked down into a storage room. There was no place for a person to be hidden. The Welsh dresser had only small cupboards below the shelves.

Jason turned away. Hurrying again, because if anyone came now and found Reece standing in a trance, there would be trouble, and delay, he went outside and over to the first shed.

Inside, it was empty and smelt of disuse. He spent one minute each on checking out the other buildings.

Cupping both hands around his mouth, Jason shouted, "Elsie!" His voice reverberated sullenly from every wall. And it got no other answer.

Slumping, Jason walked over to David Reece. Stopping beside him, he began to compose himself in order to tell the entranced man he had to forget what had happened, forget being shown a jewel.

Jason's eyes were drawn to the house. In his stomach he had that sensation of weight he always got when unsuccessfully ending one of his calls. Now the sensation was stronger.

What if there's an attic?—he mused. What if there's another room? What about the space under the stairs?

Deciding to give the whole place a second check, Jason strode back to the house and inside. First he went to the doorway on his right and looked down into the storeroom. His senses perked. He realised that the Welsh dresser was standing at an odd angle. This end touched the wall, the other end was two feet out.

Jason jumped down steps, went to the dresser, looked behind it. There a new door stood ajar, and immediately behind it another door. Jason's hope sang. It sang higher and clearer when he saw by his feet a pile of clothes, notably a blue boilersuit and rubber boots.

He tried the latch of the second door. It was locked. He pounded his fist on the wood and shouted, "Elsie! Are you there?"

At once came back a faint, "Jason! Oh God, Jason!"

He didn't know what he shouted next, or what he heard. He was too stunned, too happy. He was sensible only of his emotions. But he must have been giving out and taking in information, he realised, because he found himself running outside, going to David Reece, searching in the motionless man's pockets, not finding what he wanted, rushing back and getting a large key from the boilersuit and unlocking the door.

He flung into the room. Elsie, by a bed, was putting on her

cardigan. She dropped it and rushed to him. Again, as they embraced, Jason was unaware of what was said, of the matter of their broken sentences. His hearing dulled after Elsie's first "Darling." But he knew about the feel of her body tight in his arms, and the taste of her tears and her mouth.

---

Hull Rainer pushed through the heavy congestion of strollers. There seemed to be more of them on the sidewalk today. Which, he thought, just went to prove how badly things were going.

Hull next reprimanded himself for his pettiness. Since he was earlier today than usual, there were bound to be slight differences; and since he was in a hurry, it was only natural that his nerves would exaggerate the smallest impediment.

"Keep your cool, Albert," he mumbled.

Getting free of the stream of pedestrians, reaching the inside of the sidewalk, Hull went through swing doors and into Woolworth's. He kept his head down. As a further abnegator of recognition he was wearing sunglasses. He would have hated now what normally would give delight: being delayed by, "Excuse me, but aren't you Hull Rainer?"

He went into one of the aisles, saw ahead a concentration of shoppers around a food counter, turned with a hiss of impatience and strode to the aisle at the side.

Hull's haste and nervousness were due to the flat package which he had fixed on his belly with adhesive tape. He felt vulnerable walking around in possession of twenty-five thousand pounds in cash.

Touching his imitation pot, as he did every other minute, he mused: That traitorous bastard Reece. But at once, again, Hull countered with a soother. He told himself how clever he had been in cheating the ex-burglar, and to remember he was richer by seventy-five grand, and to relish his fooling of Wilkinson with the ransom, and—

There was a fat woman blocking the doorway to the washrooms.

Hull's face twitched. He strode on, unconscious of his

outthrust jaw and clenched fists. His mind was busily choosing harsh phrases to use in clearing the way.

At the penultimate moment, however, when Hull was within mere feet of the fat woman, she made a swift retreat into the passage and entered the ladies' room. Hull didn't even have to slow. He went through and out to the yard.

Taking off his sunglasses he replaced them with the spectacles with plain glass. Wistfully, in passing, he thought of when all this had been exciting.

Hull came out onto the alley. He stopped. An old man was there, peering into a garbage can, his lid-holding pose as elegant as if he were savouring the contents of a tureen.

Hull cleared his throat loudly, the sound an accusation. The old man glanced around, clamped down the can lid and moved away. He went to the alley's end and turned from sight.

Hull followed, as he walked bringing out and putting on the scarf and cap. He paused once to look behind. There was no tail or accidental observer.

Out on the street, two cabs stood at the rank. Crossing over the road, Hull was pleased to note that the first taxi's driver, as always before, was a new face. Little things like that mattered.

Hull got in the cab quickly. After giving his destination, he added, "And as fast as you can, please."

———◆———

Elsie and Jason had calmed—relatively. They were sitting at the table in the parlour, holding hands. Elsie was happy, disbelieving, and uneasy.

Happy: she was with Jason and he had kissed her and she was free at last from that terrible room. Disbelieving: she would not have to go through the act with her guard. Uneasy: she felt they were in danger by staying on here.

She glanced at the telephone and then through the open door at the man. He was faced the other way and without the boilersuit, an alien figure.

She asked, "Shouldn't we call the police?"

"In a minute," Jason said. "There's no hurry."

His presence and confidence, they made her relax with a smile. Her uneasiness gave way before the happy disbelief. She thought back to the miracle of rescue.

When waiting in bed for the man, wretched, Elsie had become sure as the minutes passed that this was another of his cruel tricks. She had untied her wrist. Then the knock and muffled shout had come. Although she had called out Jason's name she had not been convinced it was he, that was too much to hope for, and she knew her guard's sense of humour. She had dressed at flurrying speed because Jason it might be and, if not, she was going to call off her deal with the man. Next, the door had opened, the miracle had happened.

"I can't believe it," she said now, not for the first time.

"Neither can I," Jason said. He was looking at her. He hadn't stopped looking at her.

"It's all over."

"Yes. You're safe now. Nothing more to worry about."

"And there's no gang?"

"I'm sure there isn't," Jason said. "It's just this man Reece and the other."

Elsie gave a curious and amused frown. "You keep calling him 'the other.' Who is he, Jason?"

He glanced away, squeezed her hand, looked back and said, "This is going to be a shock. Maybe you've had enough for the time being."

"No. Please tell me. It must be someone I know well. And apart from you, I—" She stopped and shook her head. "No, that's silly."

"Go on."

"It couldn't be Hull, could it?"

"Yes," Jason said, solemn. "Everything points to that."

She smiled her bemusement. "How fantastic!"

"I know. But it's true. There is the possibility that somehow he's being forced to co-operate, but I doubt it. We can find out presently, from Reece. That's why we're not rushing away from here."

"Yes," Elsie said. She was trying to sound reasonable in the face of the absurd.

"First, though, I want to tell it to you from *my* angle, the way I've seen it from the beginning. Okay?"

"Yes, Jason."

"Sure you're all right? Sure you don't need anything?"

Elsie smiled and patted his hand. They had already been through this once. "I'm fine. Really. I haven't been hurt." Or, she thought, sullied. And she wondered if she would ever tell how close to it she had been, of her own free will.

Jason began to talk. He told of suspicion, of renting the motorcycle and following Hull, of a change of cars and appearance, of searching in this country area, of writing a letter to leave at home, of searching again and finding this place and putting the man called David Reece into a trance.

To Elsie it all sounded unreal, strange, especially with her sitting here free of the prison and that man who was standing out there like a statue.

She said, "His clothes."

"He changed into his abduction get-up only to go into your room."

"But Hull. That's what I find hardest to accept. My own husband. We were going to be divorced, yes, but this? He often said he was fond of me."

Jason nodded slowly, solemn again. "Because of your amnesia," he said, "there's something about Hull you no longer know. It might come back to you in time, with help. Could be it would be better for you to remember."

"Does he hate me? Is that what you mean?"

"No, I don't think he hates you. But I don't know."

"Then, if that's not it, why would he do this?"

"Money," Jason said, letting go of her hand and rising. "He knew of that Hollywood money on its way and wanted it. There couldn't be any other reason."

She nodded, pretending to understand the power of money. In the two months of her new life she had learned that, for most people, gold is God. And she still didn't know why.

"Back in a minute," Jason said, going to the door. "See if you can find something to drink. You need a settling shot."

Watching him go outside, Elsie thought: All I need is you. Near me. I want to be able to keep touching you.

Jason went to David Reece. He spoke to him, took his arm and turned him around. For the first time Elsie saw her captor's face. She didn't like it. A shudder ran over her.

Stepping over a shotgun lying on the ground, Jason led the man across to the house and brought him inside. To Elsie, David Reece seemed to have shrunk in height. She said so.

Jason told her, "Probably has false heels in his gumboots."

Elsie marvelled anew at the planning, the careful attention to detail, and at the fact that Hull had had it all set up when he asked to come back and stay at the apartment for a short time. She told herself to remember to congratulate him on his performance. He was quite an actor.

Jason sat the sleepwalker on a straight chair he had pulled out from the table. Taking his own chair, he put it down in front of Reece and sat facing him.

He said, "Elsie, why not see if you can rustle up some hot, sweet tea for yourself. And me."

Again Elsie felt uneasy. "Shouldn't we be hurrying this along?"

"I'm going to put him into a medium trance. It might take some time. We're safe enough."

Elsie wanted to say that at least they should close the door. She didn't. Jason knew what he was doing, she assured herself as she got up to go into the kitchen.

She couldn't find tea. While she was fixing instant coffee she heard Jason talking to David Reece in a low, insistent voice. She felt proud of Jason's skill. She felt wifely.

When Elsie entered the parlour, carrying two mugs of coffee, David Reece was saying tonelessly, "No, I don't feel any pain." Elsie knew that the depth of his trance was being tested: Jason, after telling him his hand was anesthetised, was twisting a finger.

With her coffee, Elsie stood by the table to watch. Jason leaned back and asked, "What's your name?"

"John David Reece," the man said.

"Where do you live?"

"Apple Acres, Compton Pool, Berkshire."

"Tell me how old you are, please."

"Thirty-eight last April."

Jason asked, "Are you the owner of a grey Hillman van?"

"That's right."

"And what is the name, please, of the person who is being held prisoner in your downstairs room?"

David Reece opened his mouth to answer. Nothing came out except a whine, like one produced by minor physical effort. His lips moved. He swayed forward and then back, and sat in a droop, frowning. He closed his mouth.

The frown went when Jason said soothingly, "It's all right. I don't want to know. Keep it to yourself. You're doing very well. There's nothing to worry about."

Elsie asked, "What's wrong?"

Jason slapped his knees and got up. He looked unperturbed. "A block on the open road," he said. "The straightforward approach is out. We'll have to be a bit devious." He lifted his mug and gulped at the coffee.

"I don't understand, Jason."

He finished the drink and put the mug down before answering. "One of the two big questions in hypnotism," he said, "is will or will not a subject disobey himself. Will he do, on the operator's orders, what in the waking state he would not do—for reasons moral, instinctive, religious, legal or whatever?"

"Yes," Elsie said. "I see what you mean."

"In this particular case, the reason is *il*legal, self-protective."

"He's not going to give himself away."

"Right. And I'm not going to push him. It could spoil everything. I think he's too much of a crook to give in. We'll try another approach."

Jason returned to the chair, facing David Reece. He said to

him, "In front of you, by your right hand, is a telephone. Do you see it?"

"A telephone?"

"Yes. It's right there. A regular black telephone. If you concentrate really hard you'll be able to see it. The light is poor in here but you have excellent vision. There, now you see it."

David Reece nodded. "Yes."

"In a moment," Jason said, "someone you know is going to call. Hull Rainer. You will be pleased to hear from him. Even though his voice sounds different, you will know it is Hull Rainer because you can't be fooled. You and he will chat. Ah, there goes the call signal. Pick up the receiver."

David Reece moved his right hand forward, made a grasping motion, raised the clawed hand to a position by the side of his face. He smiled faintly. "Hello?"

In his usual voice, Jason said, "Hello. Hull here. How are you keeping?"

Reece said, "In good form. How's things with you, mate?"

"Couldn't be better," Jason said. He asked about the weather, asked about the farm—Reece giving conversational answers—and then said, "You know, I was thinking today about the first time you and I met. In Brighton, on the pier."

The man shook his head firmly. "No, not Brighton. You must be thinking of someone else. It was in London."

"Was it?"

"Sure, Hull boy. Outside the Lyceum theatre. You had some tickets to sell. Remember now?"

"Of course," Jason said. "Good for you. You're clever to recall things like that. Not many can. Real clever. Yes, that's where we met. But I bet you can't remember what I was working in then."

"Sure I can. Easy. You was in that play, acting a sailor."

"So I was. A good part."

David Reece said, "That's not what you told me then."

"You know what actors're like," Jason said easily. "But I admire your memory. Let's see how good it really is, shall we?"

"Fine. Go ahead."

Elsie listened in fascination as Jason, carefully and with frequent compliments, drew out of David Reece the association between himself and Hull. There were times when a crafty look came over the man's face; obviously he was holding back things he had never told Hull in the waking state and therefore wouldn't now.

From fewer questions, more of Reece's corrections to Jason's deliberate mistakes, Elsie heard of Hull's recent approach with a proposition, the plan for her abduction, its implementation, the ransom of fifty thousand pounds.

"I have to ring off now," Jason said. "Be seeing you."

"Sure. See you soon. 'Bye." Reece lowered his hand.

Jason leaned back with a sigh. He and Elsie looked at each other, both shaking their heads. Elsie said, "What a story. I still find it incredible."

"So do I. Even though it's what I had in mind right from the start."

"And what's the next move, Jason?"

"Tie him up. Bring him out of his trance. Call the police."

"Good," Elsie said, relieved. "I think there's rope in the storage room."

In five minutes, David Reece had his hands tied together behind the chair back and was being brought out of his trance. He sat facing the door. Elsie stood by the rear wall.

Jason returned his chair to the table, turned and snapped his fingers, which was the signal for disentrancement he had given to his subject. David Reece jerked his head. After staring up at Jason briefly, he tried to stand. He fell back, snarling:

"What the hell's this?"

"Relax," Jason said coldly. "The caper's over. Elsie's free and you're caught."

"What—who—?"

"I'm Jason Galt, if the name means anything to you. I'm a hypnotist. I put you to sleep and you sang very prettily for us."

Reece sneered. "Oh, sure."

Jason repeated three of the incidents the man had described. He added, "Yesterday afternoon you didn't go out, you had a beer here with Rainer, but you did drive out in the evening, to make the call to the telephone booth. Shall I tell you more?"

Elsie went forward and stood beside Jason. The man glared at her before nodding slowly, looking down and darting his gaze around the floor. His puffy mouth was grim.

"Please call the police," Elsie said. She wanted this to be over. One of the many things she hated about it was her feeling of triumph.

Jason went toward the telephone.

He stopped at the same moment as Elsie turned her head, and for the same reason. Approaching in the near distance was the sound of a car.

Jason looked at his watch. "A bit early for Hull. Who is it, Reece?"

The man in the chair made no answer. He was twisting his hands against the rope.

Elsie gasped, "The gun!"

Jason darted outside. He ran to the shotgun and picked it up and hurried back in the parlour. Leaving the door ajar, he strode to the window and looked out. Quickly he moved aside.

"It's Hull," he snapped. "Elsie, keep out of sight."

She moved to a corner of the room and crouched down. Jason, kneeling and aiming the gun at Reece, said, "Lovely. We'll have the pair of you. Is Rainer armed?"

Again the man said nothing. Jason hefted the gun. "Never mind. You just do as I tell you, say what I want you to say, and you'll live long enough to serve time."

---

Hull brought the Ford to a stop in the yard. He switched off the motor with a grunt of satisfaction at having arrived safely. Opening the door he began to get out—and froze.

Some yards away, leaning against a building, was a motorcycle. Hull stared at it. He saw a vapour of heat rising from its engine. The machine had not been here long. Listening, he looked around the property.

All appeared to be normal. The silence did seem to have an unusual depth to it, but the house door stood open, as was often the case, and smoke was trailing up out of the chimney.

Now, from the house, came David Reece's voice, calling, "Hello there. Come in. You're early."

That seemed okay, Hull mused. He went the rest of the way out of the car. Its door he left wide. He felt not alarmed but wary, superwary. His thought was: Don't like that bloody bike.

"Come on in," Reece called.

Hull answered, "Yes. A minute." There was something about a motorcycle that was tickling his memory. He couldn't nail it down. Had he seen one around a little too often—that could be it.

Hull called out, "Who owns the bike?"

There was a short, odd pause—making Hull frown—before Reece said, "*I* do."

"Since when?"

"This morning." Pause. "I bought it." Pause. "Be taking a trip when all this is over."

Could be, Hull thought. Another thought led him to call, "Why don't you come out?"

A pause, and, "I'm washing my feet."

Hull shrugged in acceptance. He told himself he was getting paranoid. He too could do with a trip, a nice long vacation. There were thousands of motorbikes around, and Reece's voice sounded odd and hesitant because he was bending over giving his feet a wash. It was so easy to jump to wild conclusions.

Giving a pat to the money that lay snug against his stomach, Hull began to move toward the house. He took off his cap, folded it and put it in a pocket, did the same with his glasses, loosened the scarf.

He reached the doorstep. After a last, dismissing glance back at the motorcycle, he went into the parlour.

In a jumble of startling images which came so fast that he gasped and raised a shielding hand, Hull saw a sitting Reece with footwear normal, saw his wife Elsie crouching in a corner, saw the grimness of Reece's face and the way his arms were pulled back out of sight, saw rising from under the window Jason Galt, saw the shotgun in Galt's hands.

Hull whispered, "Oh, my God," and in spite of everything wore enough shreds of his vanity-raiment to hope nobody heard. He felt ill.

"Don't move," Jason Galt said, pointing the shotgun. "Search him, Elsie."

"What?" she asked.

"See if he has a gun. Pat him under the arms and around the waist."

Elsie rose and came forward. She looked at Hull like a stranger. He said a feeble and obvious, "I can explain." Elsie went behind him and Galt ordered, "Lift your arms, Rainer."

Hull obeyed. He felt his wife's hands fumble about his jacket. She said, "No, nothing."

Jason Galt came closer. He still held the shotgun at the ready. His face showed a quiet hate. He said, "You're a real sweet guy."

"Look. You're making a mistake."

"Of course we are. When your pal Reece told us the whole thing under hypnosis we didn't believe a word of it. And I'm certainly mistaken about the church, Woolworth's, the disguise, the taxi, the Odeon parking lot."

"There's an explanation."

"Of course, of course."

Act, Hull was urging himself. Perform. Play the astounded innocent. Put the blame on Reece. Say he's a liar.

But Hull couldn't take the expression of cowed guilt off his face, he couldn't stop staring at the two mammoth-looking holes at the shotgun end, and he couldn't keep the tremble out of his voice.

"Believe me, Galt, you've got it all wrong. Elsie?"

She had gone back to the other side of the room. She wouldn't look at him. "Jason," she said. "Let's call the police now."

David Reece spoke. He was sitting erect, alert. His eyes on Hull, he hissed, "Jump him."

Hull, nervously: "Eh?"

"Jump him, you fool. The gun's not loaded."

Could there be a chance, Hull wondered. But as he looked measuringly at Galt, rapidly computing age, height and weight differences, the hypnotist turned the shotgun on Reece with:

"Let's see if it's loaded or not."

Flinching, Reece blurted, "It is, it's loaded."

"Which barrel?"

"Both, both."

Galt moved the gun back to cover Hull, who hoped once more when he heard Elsie say, "Darling." He quickly sent her an eager-wistful glance, only to see that she was addressing the hypnotist.

"Darling," she said again. "The police."

"Right," Galt said. He ordered, "Rainer, step backwards to the door. Reach behind you and close it. Lean on it and put your hands on your head."

Hull obeyed in every detail. He was telling himself that everything was going to be all right, that nothing really bad could happen, not to him, not to Albert. Even so, standing with hands on head, Hull was petrified and ashamed.

Galt started to move forward, making to come past and go to the telephone. He drew abreast. His back was to David Reece, who sat some six feet away.

Hull saw it coming. He couldn't stop his face from reacting. Galt saw that. He began to turn, but too late.

To Hull, the action was as if it were being done in slow motion: David Reece getting up, the chair still at his back, and coming forward in a stoop. It seemed to take long minutes for him to reach Galt and butt him in the ribs with his head.

In reality it happened so fast, Reece's move a swift charge, that Galt was falling toward Hull at the same time as Elsie was screaming a warning of the attack.

Hull shot out both hands to share with Galt a grip on the gun. His head collided with the taller man's face. Galt automatically sprang his right hand free of the stock and put it to the blood beside his eye. Hull twisted to the side, trying to break the gun loose from the remaining hand.

Elsie came running forward to help the hypnotist. David Reece, still bent over, swung around and crashed into her with the chair. She cried out as she stumbled away.

Her cry made Galt glance around. Blood was running down his face and edging between his fingers. He seemed, briefly, to be more interested in Elsie's welfare than in possession of the weapon.

Hull gave a mighty side-wrench. The shotgun came free of Galt's hold; came also free, the wrench so strong, from Hull's own hands. It went flying across the room. It hit the wall and fell to the floor.

Jason Galt made to follow. Hull grabbed him. It was not so much containment as the need to grab, to hold on to something. The violence he was involved in was taking him close to tears. The sight of the blood gave him the taste of vomit.

"Gun, Elsie!" the hypnotist shouted. "Get it!"

There was a grotesque, crouching, scrambling race between Elsie and David Reece. At the same time they arrived in the area of the shotgun. Elsie stooped lower, reaching. Reece surged sideways and knocked her staggering.

Jason Galt tried to pull free. The struggle between him and Hull was a manic skirmish of hands. Continually, every other second, Hull's grips on the other man's windcheater, arms, and shirt were broken and regained.

None of the four people were speaking. The only sounds in the room were the clatter and thud of movement, the grunts of effort and the rasp of laboured breathing.

Recovering from her stagger, Elsie turned and rushed back. Reece had just taken up a crouching stand over the shotgun, the chair still perched crazily on his back. He was weaving his head: a weapon.

Elsie dodged in her rush. As she went by she grabbed Reece's hair. She swung him around and with her free hand brought up a hard slap. It got Reece on the face. He went up and back, sat on the chair, went farther back, was prevented from falling over by hitting the wall.

Elsie dove toward the gun. Her hands reached it as her knees were struck by the outstretched feet of the man on the chair. She gasped with pain, fell and rolled, left the gun behind.

Hull was holding on grimly to the windcheater. Jason Galt gave up trying to push him away. Keeping his left hand in place on Hull's shoulder, he took his right arm away and drew it far back. He threw a punch.

It caught Hull on the side of his jaw. The pain caused him to gag and whimper. Hold unbroken, he yanked himself in closer. Again his head hit the taller man's face. Hull felt the wet of blood on his brow.

Reece, having pushed off the wall, had straddled the shotgun with the legs of the chair. He was sitting with his own legs raised and bent, the feet poised like fists.

Now, as Elsie came rushing back to the attack, he kicked out against her unco-ordinated slaps and grabs. Two kicks were lucky: one got her elbow, the other her thigh. She went stumbling backwards.

To Hull, Reece shouted, "Get away from him! Get over here!"

"I'm trying," Hull panted, holding on tight. "Trying."

The hypnotist drew back his arm again. He threw another punch. Behind it was all the weight of his swinging body. The fist scraped without harm past the back of Hull's head; but the forearm made solid contact.

Although Hull lost his hold and was knocked away, he was sent in the direction of David Reece. He weaved there and finished up on his knees beside the chair.

Reece snarled, "The gun."

Hull dithered his hands between the legs and spindles. He got hold of the weapon. He tried to pull it out. A leg intervened.

Jason Galt shouted, "Out, Elsie, out!" He pulled the door wide open. His face was streaked with blood.

Hull got the shotgun out and into both hands. Still on his knees he turned toward the door. There, Galt was being joined at a run by Elsie. Her face was wild and white.

Reece screamed, "Shoot!"

Hull said weakly, "I can't."

His wife and the hypnotist ran out.

"You bastard," David Reece raged. "Untie me. Quick."

Hull dropped the gun. He got up and leaned behind the chair. His fingers trembled at the knots in the rope.

"A knife," Reece snapped. "The kitchen."

Hull ran into the kitchen and saw an open drawer and grabbed up a knife. On his way back he heard from outside Jason Galt urgently ordering Elsie, "Keep running. I'll catch you up."

Hull, tasting vomit again, slashed at the rope. Under pressure from straining hands, it burst apart. David Reece leapt up, grabbed the gun, sped to the door.

———◆▶————

Elsie was running the wrong way.

Jason shouted, "The track's here! Between those sheds!"

She changed course. Jason, astride the motorcycle, kicked viciously at the starter pedal. His heart pained as the engine roared to life.

Elsie went from sight between the two buildings, and David Reece appeared. He came bursting from the house. He had the shotgun. Stopping, he raised it to his shoulder and sighted on Jason.

It was too late to drive away. Jason leapt off the machine. He was flinging himself to the ground when Reece fired. Jason's snarling yell at the hot stabs of pain in his leg was drowned by two noises.

First, a wild clatter as the main body of the buckshot hit the motorcycle; next, two seconds later, the ear-shattering crash as the gas tank exploded.

Still rolling from his fall, Jason was buffeted further by the explosion. Bits of flame peppered his clothes. He rolled on and got behind the Ford.

Incredibly, the pain in his left leg had dulled. He got up in a crouch, patting the fire spots on his pants and jacket. He was dazed.

Nearby, the motorcycle burned with bright intensity. White and orange flames shot up at odd angles. The mass of metal was spitting and crackling. Black smoke rose lazily.

Peering through the car windows, Jason could see David Reece backing away from the fire, an arm shielding his face. Farther on, toward the house, Hull Rainer stood holding a knife.

A billow of smoke drifted across the yard. Jason turned and ran. He had a limp. The pain returned to needle life every time he put weight on his leg. He reckoned he had caught five or six pellets.

He got safely out of the yard. Coming out beyond the buildings, he saw Elsie on the track. She was thirty feet away but running in his direction, her face anguished.

"All right?" she gasped.

Jason nodded. He was about to tell her to turn, run on. But he saw that ahead the terrain was clear for two hundred yards. There was no hope of reaching cover before David Reece came up behind.

"This way," he said. "Quickly."

Elsie reached him as he veered off the track. Running, they clasped hands. Jason steered Elsie close to the nearest building. He had no fear that the sound of their running would be heard.

From the yard came the hiss and crackle of fire. There was a smell of petrol. Smoke was streaming up over the rooftops.

Jason and Elsie, behind the buildings, paused at a corner. Cautiously Jason looked through into the yard. He saw no one. He pulled Elsie across the space to the next shed, and then on to the next, which was the last.

The farm lay behind. Ahead was a broad field. It ended a hundred feet away against a line of trees, the first of a wood. The wood looked dense.

"We can make it," Jason gasped.

Elsie said, "Yes."

The ground was hard. Too hard. Every time Jason's left foot slammed down, the pain seared. He gritted his teeth and took to making long strides on his right leg.

Elsie asked, "What's wrong?"

"Nothing. Keep running."

After saying which, Jason trod on a stone. It was his damaged leg. Each buried pellet screamed its agony. He cried out, his leg gave way, he fell.

Elsie also cried out. She bent over him. She said a distraught, "Your shoe's soaked with blood."

Panting, Jason told her, "Got me with buckshot. One or two. It's nothing to—"

"He's there!"

Jason jerked his head the other way. From around one of the buildings the two men were running, Reece in the lead.

Elsie: "Can you get up?"

He could. He did. He began a limping run, Elsie at his side. He looked behind. David Reece had stopped and was aiming the shotgun.

Jason didn't hesitate. He gave Elsie a violent push, shouted for her to drop, and dropped himself.

The shot sounded. Simultaneously, it seemed, there was a whistling in the air overhead, a spattering in the earth, and a hard tap on the sole of one of Jason's shoes.

He asked, "All right?"

Elsie panted, "Yes."

"Up!" he said. "Run!"

They got up and ran. Jerking out the words, Elsie said, "That's the second barrel. Maybe he has no more shells."

They were nearly at the trees. Jason forged on, face tight

against the pain. He and Elsie looked back. David Reece was bringing something from his pocket as he ran; the gun was broken open. He had more shells.

The trees. Jason and Elsie went quickly into the gloom beneath the evergreen foliage, went on until the trunks they passed began to blot them from view.

Jason pulled Elsie to a stop behind a tree with a thick bole. They were both gasping for breath. They peered through to the field.

David Reece was approaching at a brisk jog. His shotgun was closed again. His face was grimly confident. Hull Rainer, surprisingly, was running back the other way.

Elsie whispered, "What's Hull doing?"

"No idea."

She turned to him. "Jason, are we going to be all right?"

"Of course."

"I'm so sorry I got you into this."

"I'm not," he said. "I'm glad I'm with you."

"If only we'd called the police as soon as you found me."

Because she'd be hurt, Jason couldn't tell her what he was ashamed of, that thinking there was a possibility she could be involved, despite appearances, he'd had to find out the truth first from Reece; then, if needs be, he could have arranged to keep the police out of it.

He said, "Come on. He's getting close."

They ran on. Jason took Elsie's hand and led her around so that they were moving level with the front of the trees. He signalled for a stop. After halting, they listened.

From behind came sounds of movement. From beyond the trees came the whine of a starter followed by a car's motor being revved. Jason whispered, "Hull. He's bringing the car."

"What for?"

"Catch us in the middle, I suppose. And chase us if we make a break for the open."

Elsie came close, whispering, "What shall we do?"

"Play for time. Someone might've heard that explosion and come to investigate."

The sounds from behind were fainter. Elsie said, "Let me look at your leg." Sinking to her knees she pulled up the leg of his jeans. Jason bent to see. On his calf were spread four swellings, each with a centre hole, each with a trail of dried blood.

"I'll live," he said. "Come on. Go as quietly as you can."

They went on softly. Elsie whispered, "I'm glad you're not scared. It makes me feel better."

Jason was scared only of Reece and Rainer's hastiness. If he could get them to settle and talk, he could produce the ticket to safety: the carbon of his letter.

He reminded Elsie of it as they walked. She squeezed his hand and smiled. He was proud of her courage.

They were closer now to the edge of the wood. Between trunks they could glimpse the field. Jason saw flashes of the green Ford as it came bouncing over the ground.

He changed course again, leading Elsie deeper into the trees. She wanted to stop so she could wipe the blood off his face. He kept her moving. He had no pain from the cuts he could feel by his eye and inside his bottom lip.

Presently they saw slits of light through the trees. They were nearing the far side of the wood. They hurried on. They heard the car stop somewhere to the left. Reece, Jason figured, must be over to the right.

The trees thinned out. Beyond lay a vast, open stretch of countryside. It was flat, without buildings, and almost treeless. Even worse, it was ploughed, crossways. Running would be near impossible—if there were any cover to run to.

Jason and Elsie went back into the gloom. They stopped to listen. From Reece's end, the east, came sounds of fast walking. From the other end they heard nothing.

"This way," Jason hissed. He moved to the west. Hull Rainer, he knew, would be the easiest of the two to handle, and not only because the shotgun was with the other man.

As if reading his mind, Elsie asked in a whisper, "What if he got a gun from the house?"

"I'm banking on there being only one. Reece's. Keep moving."

Not holding hands now, using their arms like tightrope walkers, they went on at a creeping pace. The sounds from behind grew fainter. Reece, Jason thought, was probably beating back and forth across the narrow strip of woodland.

They came to a sloping bank, head-height. It acted as a barrier against near sound, for not until they were halfway up the slope, treading softly, did they hear the footfalls.

Jason signalled Elsie to wait. He went on, dropping to his hands. Carefully he peered over the top. Hull Rainer was there, ten feet away, walking noisily from one clump of bushes to another—the knife, blade up, in his hand.

Jason looked at the ground beside him. He saw a stone. He picked it up, rose slightly and took aim on a spot just beyond where Rainer was searching. He threw.

His aim was good. The stone clattered on a tree trunk and fell loudly in the cold-crackly flora.

Hull whirled to face that direction. His knife at the ready, he backed away. He backed toward the bank. He said, "I see you."

Jason got up quickly but softly. One long stride on his sound leg took him to the summit. Another stride of the same measure and same side took him midway down the slope. He held his breath. And he overbalanced.

Rainer jerked around at the noise. He stared, he waved the knife, he yelled, "Dave! This way!"

Jason got up. He put out his hands, palms down in a gesture of peace. Urgently he said, "Listen. You're in trouble. Stop a minute and listen. If anything happens to us you're in big trouble."

"Quick, Dave!" Rainer shouted. "Hurry!" He moved forward threateningly. "Don't pull anything, Galt."

"Will you listen a minute, you fool?"

Elsie appeared on top of the bank. "He's serious, Hull," she said. "Let him tell you."

Rainer directed his face away to shout, "Dave!"

Jason leapt. He had two yards to cover. It was one stride on his good leg. He reached the actor, feinted with his left toward the knife and threw in a long straight right. It made contact. Hull Rainer went staggering backwards and fell in a sprawl.

Jason snapped, "Let's go."

He and Elsie began to run. They ran without caution, careless of the noise they were making. They ran faster when they heard Rainer call shrilly for David Reece.

Elsie tripped. She fell, rolled, got up before Jason could reach her to help, sped on again.

They were nearing the edge of the wood. Jason had lost track of direction, didn't know if they were heading north, south or west, but he did know they weren't heading east, and that was good enough.

Elsie, moving along at his side, gasped, "The car!" She pointed.

Rainer's rented Ford stood along the tree line. Jason followed Elsie as she changed course, heading for the car, and thought: If the key's in . . .

The trees ended. They were out in the open. They dashed to the Ford and Jason yanked open the driver's door. The key was in the ignition. He said, "In, in. Quick."

They got inside. Both were panting from the run, their chests heaving. Elsie rolled down her window while Jason switched on and looked for the starter button. He couldn't see one.

He realised it could be on the key itself. He turned it further around and was rewarded by the starter's whine. The motor caught. He raced it. And he swung his head fast when David Reece said, "Freeze."

The black nostrils of the shotgun were aimed at Elsie, held an inch from her face. She sat rigid, staring straight ahead. Reece was smiling and breathing heavily.

Hull Rainer came up behind. He said, "Him. He's the one to cover."

"Can't you see how it is between them?" Reece asked. "Are

you blind?" He told Jason, "Switch off, friend, or the lady loses her face."

Carefully, terrified of making a move that would cause the man to overreact, Jason reached to the key. He turned it and killed the motor.

"That's better," Reece said. "Now you, Elsie, you get out nice and slow and come in the back with me."

Jason told her. "Do what he wants, exactly what he wants." He put his hands in clear view at the top of the steering wheel.

Elsie opened the door, got out, opened the back door, climbed in and slid across the seat, her movements like those of a robot. The snout of the gun was never far from her face. Reece sat beside her. Rainer got in the front.

David Reece ordered, "Drive."

Jason asked, "May I tell you something for your own good?"

"No."

"I don't know what the sentence is for kidnapping, but for murder you get life."

"Mate, you're a mine of information."

"The authorities will know I came here today."

"Sure," Reece said. "You told the milkman and ten other people. That's an old gag."

Jason shook his head. "I left a letter. If Rainer cares to reach into my hip pocket he'll find the carbon copy."

David Reece sneered, "You wrote someone my address and phone number, eh? The hell you did. You didn't know you were coming here. It was a lucky call."

"Read the letter," Jason said. He looked at Rainer as he eased his hips off the seat. The actor's face was drawn and pale. His forehead was speckled with dry blood like flat scabs. A pulse throbbed at the side of his neck.

"Please, Hull," Elsie said. "Read it."

David Reece, impatiently: "Go ahead, get the bloody letter."

Rainer reached into the pocket and brought out the piece of

paper. As he unfolded it, Jason said, "The original's in a safe place, in an envelope marked 'To Whom It May Concern.'"

The actor's eyes were skipping back and forth across the words. Reece told him to read aloud. Rainer did so. His eyes grew anxious, his voice low, his reading hesitant. Even when he had finished he went on looking at the paper.

David Reece told him grimly, "You and your smart ideas."

Rainer mumbled, "This changes things."

"It does if we don't get that original."

"You can't," Elsie said defiantly. "It's not here."

Reece's eyes met Jason's in the rearview mirror. The man with the gun asked, "Where's the original?"

Jason was about to say that it was with his lawyer. Elsie spoke first, still defiant. She said, "In his flat."

Jason closed his eyes. He drooped forward until his face touched his hands. While Hull Rainer said a bewildered, "Thank you," and David Reece chuckled, Jason bemoaned the fact that Elsie was too unschooled in crime fiction to fully understand the gambit. Any twelve-year-old would know it through reading and television. Elsie had known once, but it had gone with her memory. He had destroyed it himself.

---

The man at her side said, "That makes things easier all round." Elsie didn't understand what he meant, nor why he was looking so smug, nor why Jason appeared to have given up hope.

Possibly, she thought, David Reece was being ironic and Jason was relaxing in relief.

She said, "So now you can't kill us."

No one answered her. Reece was asking Hull if he knew Jason's address, and her husband, that strange man, said, "Yes. Thank God."

"He would've told us anyway," David Reece said. He tapped the gun on Elsie's shoulder. "He's going to co-operate beautifully, aren't you, Galt?"

Jason lifted his head, sat up. "Yes."

"I like a bit of co-operation. Give Rainer the key to your place. Do it slowly. Keep one hand in view."

Jason complied. As her husband accepted the leather key-holder, Elsie began to understand about the letter. She huddled over a shrinking sensation in her chest.

"Galt," Reece asked, "where is that envelope exactly?"

"Living-room table," Jason said in a monotone.

"Good."

In a livelier voice Jason said, "A farmer. Near here. Big family. I think he's a poacher. He knows I came here. He gave me directions."

"That's all right. I can handle old George. He's no lover of the law. But how come you asked for directions?"

"The landlord of The Jolly Miller and a customer. That's two more who know. They gave me names. I told them I was looking for a green Ford."

"Well, that's okay too. When we've got the letter, no one's going to know about this car."

Hull put the folded paper in his pocket and glanced around. "We have to talk about this, Dave."

"Shurrup," Reece said. "Let's get back to the house. You, Galt, drive on. Nice and slow. I wouldn't want my finger to get jolted."

Jason started the car. He eased it forward as if carrying eggs. Elsie wanted to shout at him to go fast, to run, to do whatever he liked. She was too wretched for speech. And she was horrifyingly conscious of the two evil holes near her face.

No one spoke during the short, crawling drive. The motor hummed, the bodywork whined and ticked. The four people might have been friends out for a sociable drive, Elsie thought. In appearance, at any rate. The atmosphere was achingly tight.

"See," Reece said to her. "I told you it was a nice day."

Which was ludicrous. It added to the quality of unreality. She wondered if she would wake up in a minute to find herself on the bed in her cellar prison.

The car came to the farm. Jason steered into the yard,

stopped, switched off. Nearby lay the motorcycle. It was a mess of twisted blackness. One tyre was burning, sending up a column of blue-grey smoke.

"That'll be seen for miles," Hull said.

David Reece told him, "It's not too important. Out here we burn our own garbage. Anyway, best to put it out. You'll find a shovel in that shed. Put dirt on the tyre."

Hull nodded meekly. "Yes."

"All right, Galt," the man with the gun said. "Get out and go stand by the house door. No tricks, mind."

"No tricks."

Elsie watched sadly as Jason left the car and walked over to the house. She felt the way he appeared to feel, as suggested by his movements—broken, hopeless.

Of the man at her side she asked, "What are you going to do with us?"

"No questions. Get out."

Hull was already at work with a shovel by the time Elsie reached Jason, who, on Reece's orders, went on in front through the parlour and the storage room and into the cellar.

"You too," David Reece said. "In you go."

Elsie hung back. "He's hurt. You shot him. Could you give me something for his wounds?"

Reece twisted his thick lips in a grin. "What're you offering in trade, dearie?"

"Whatever you want. If you mean it."

He laughed and gave her a push. "Get in there."

She went into the prison room. The door slammed behind her and was locked. She crossed straight to the corner, poured out fresh water into the basin, took it with soap and towel to where Jason was sitting on the bed. He looked exhausted. Yet he smiled, saying:

"Cheer up. Where there's life, y'know."

"Yes, I know." She knelt at his feet. "We're going to be all right."

He touched her hair. "Yes, we'll be fine. We'll get out of this little mess."

"I'm sorry," she said. "The letter."

"It's not your fault. It's mine."

She looked up at him. "How?"

"Someday I'll tell you," he said softly. "Let's forget it for the time being."

Elsie eased up the leg of his jeans. She washed the ugly, holed bumps. Next she rose and cleaned the blood from his face. The outside cut, near his eye, was small. She coated it with soap.

"Now lie down," she said. "Rest."

He moved back on the bed. "Rest with me."

They lay down together, in each other's arms, their heads close. Elsie sighed with comfort, satisfaction, and . . .

"Jason," she said. "I love you."

"I love you too, Elsie."

———◆———

The smoke had ended, smothered with dirt.

Hull let the shovel fall from his hand. He felt weak, a wreck. His body was worn out, his nerves were in shreds. He had just been through the worst half hour of his life, a period which had seemed as long as a day.

He had suffered every downbeat emotion. His strongest emotion now, as he drooped into the house, was amazement that he was still able to function. He expected at any moment to fall in a gibbering heap.

David Reece stood by the fireplace, the shotgun over his arm. He said without preliminaries, "They've got to die."

Hull twitched. To hide his face he turned away and closed the door. He said, "No, Dave."

"No? Don't give me No. You want them to walk away from here and go straight to the nearest copper?"

Turning back, Hull went to a chair. He sagged into it tiredly. "Maybe they'd agree to keep quiet if we spared their lives."

"Jesus Christ," Reece said. "You're a bigger fool than I thought. You mean you'd be willing to let 'em go if they promised nicely not to talk?"

"Well—"

"They have to die. That's that."

"Dave," Hull said weakly. "You can't just kill two people."

"Right. Right when you say *you*, meaning me. I'm going to deal with one, you are going to deal with the other."

"Eh?"

David Reece said, "That's why I didn't shoot before, at the car. We've got to get this settled. We're in it together. It's fifty-fifty. Half the money, half the dirty work."

Hull, shaking his head, was not attempting to hide his horror. "No, Dave, no. God Almighty, no."

"You want to spend the next few years inside?" Reece asked harshly and angrily. "The best years of your life? Sure you do. Wake up, mate."

"But murder. *Murder*."

"That's a word for books and newspapers. Soldiers don't use it, nor spies, nor executioners. This is a killing. Self-defence. You'd shoot someone that was going to stick a knife in you, wouldn't you?"

"But no one is, Dave. It's not self-defence."

Reece nodded, calming. "Yes, it is. Maybe you've never seen anyone who's served a long sentence. *I* have. Better these two dead than us the walking dead."

"No, Dave."

"Look. It's money and freedom against nothing and prison. Figure it out for yourself."

Hull was still shaking his head. "No."

The expression in the ex-burglar's eyes was half hate, half pity. He nodded, looked down at the gun, said quietly, "You best start thinking straight. I'm not going inside." He stroked the gun barrel. "I'll kill three times first."

Hull felt nauseated. He knew Reece wouldn't hesitate to carry out that threat. With the three of them out of the way Reece would be safe, be the loner he had always been. There would be little to connect him with the kidnapping. He could dump the Ford somewhere in London, get the letter, and be clean.

"Dave, listen," Hull said unsteadily. "There's got to be a way out of this. I'll think of something."

Reece looked up. "Only one way, Hull boy. Then we'll be golden. I'll bury the motorbike, you get the letter and return the car to the hire firm. That's all."

"The Jolly Miller," Hull warned. "The landlord and the customer."

"Nothing. Just a man looking for a car, and there'd be nothing to connect you with a green Ford."

"There will, you. Galt got your name there."

"If anyone asks, which they won't, I'll say the man never came here." Reece moved forward with his free hand out. "Give us that carbon."

Hull passed the page over. Watching Reece take it to the hearth and throw it in the flames, he said, "We could still tell them it was a joke."

Turning, David Reece shook his head and hissed with impatience. "Christ, mate, it's too late for those covering stories—a joke, a shock for Elsie's memory. There's a man in there that's been shot, a woman that's been kept prisoner for days. Straighten out your brain and—"

"Memory!" Hull blurted. He lifted his shoulders. "Elsie's memory."

"What?"

"Listen. I think I've got something. Wait. Wait a minute."

"What the hell you talking about?"

Hull got up and began to pace. He blinked constantly. One hand fumbled at his chin, the other was held to his neck. He said, half to himself:

"Jason Galt. Hypnotist. What if he could put Elsie into a trance and make her forget this past half hour, the time from his arrival here? It's possible. By God, it is. So then all she'd know is what she knew before—a man in coveralls and a barely furnished cellar."

Hull stopped abruptly and turned on Reece. "You see!"

"Sort of. What next?"

"That's it. We release her as planned. She can only tell what she could before."

"If it worked," David Reece said. "And we wouldn't know that till she'd talked."

Hull leaned forward eagerly. "Yes, we would. Look. After Galt brings her out of the trance we'll test her. You talk to her, alone. She won't know you if it's worked. And you can ask her the questions the police will. It's *good*, Dave!"

"Sounds tricky. And what about her seeing me when I talk to her?"

"Galt puts her into another trance and makes her forget *that*."

"Very tricky."

"It's worth trying. It's better than killing, if it comes off. We'll have pulled the caper after all and won't have the threat of a murder charge hanging over us."

Reece nodded. "Yes, but you're forgetting one thing."

"What's that?"

"Galt himself."

"You mean he won't play along, hypnotise her and make her forget?"

"No," Reece said. "I mean he'll still have to be dealt with. We couldn't let him go."

"Oh," Hull said flatly. His eagerness seeped away. Going back to the chair he said, "You're right."

"Still, one to do in is better than two."

"Perhaps we could pay him to keep quiet."

David Reece said, "You're dreaming again, Hull boy. Our trust apart, he wouldn't do that and he wouldn't go away. He's in love with Elsie. No, he has to die—if this thing works. One of us has to kill him."

Hull shook his head. "Dave, don't talk that way. I couldn't kill anything."

After a pause, Reece said, "I might do your half of the job. For a price." Hull said nothing. The other man went on, "Which reminds me, did you bring it?"

"It?"

"The money, mate. My share. My twenty-five thousand pounds."

His movements flaccid, Hull pulled open his shirt and worked free the packet taped to his stomach. Not until he had handed over the money did he realise he could have guaranteed his own safety by saying he'd left it at home. He didn't care.

Reece was opening the packet on the table. He said, crooning as if over a kitten, "Mm, look at that. What a pretty sight. Mostly new and crispy and clean. Twenty-five yards of lovely lawn. And that's only the half of it."

Hull watched in silence. He was faintly disgusted, faintly fascinated. Reece, while stacking and unstacking the wads, continued in a more normal tone and as if musing aloud:

"For the other half a man would do a lot. He'd do another man's job, in fact. Half of it. There you are, a half for a half. He'd do the job and the fella need never know about it—when it was done or how or where. He needn't get his little hands soiled. It would be worth the extra risk."

David Reece glanced over at Hull, who nodded slightly to show he was following, understanding. Reece went on:

"Either that or the hypnosis idea is off and the fella kills his own bird. I don't like the trance bit anyway. She could remember sometime, in a week or a month. Still, I could've gone abroad by then if I felt like it. With another twenty-five thousand I could do anything."

Hull said abruptly, "Ten thousand."

Reece ended the game. He wrapped the money roughly and took the bundle into the kitchen. At once he was back again. Coldly he said, "All or nothing. The other twenty-five grand, and I'll see to Jason Galt. *If* Elsie passes the test."

Hull rose from the chair. Keeping his eyes down, he said quietly, "It's a deal."

———◆———

There was the sound of a key poking into the lock. Jason and Elsie sat up as the door opened. In came David Reece.

He was holding the shotgun. Smiling, he said, "That looks real cozy."

Elsie swung her legs to the floor. Jason shuffled forward and did the same. He felt rested now, alert. The enfeebling sickness that had stricken him when the gun had been pointed at Elsie's face had gone.

"Looks like you two have been having a nice old time here," Reece said. When they didn't answer, he stopped smiling. "Come with me, Galt."

Jason, watching the man carefully, asked, "Why?"

"You'll see. Come on."

Elsie gripped Jason's arm. "No. Don't go."

David Reece asked, "Do you or do you not want to live?"

Jason: "Of course we do."

"Then come with me. We've got an idea that might work. It's the only chance for the pair of you."

"What is it?"

"We'll explain. It all depends on you." He moved the gun's snout slightly, bringing it to an aim on Elsie. "Come on, Galt, up you get."

"Don't go, darling," Elsie said urgently. "Let's stay together."

Jason freed her hand. "I'll have to see what this idea is. Don't worry. They're as much concerned about their safety as we are about ours."

Looking miserable, Elsie subsided. Jason kissed her cheek, got up and crossed the room. He limped. His leg was stiff from the knee down.

Reece stood back. "Go ahead of me." He was close behind Jason, touching his lower spine with the gun, as they went through the two doors. After the first was locked, they went on up to the parlour.

Hull Rainer was standing by the window. He glanced around and then went back to gazing outside. His attitude suggested he wished he were out there and far away.

"Sit on that chair," Reece ordered.

Jason sat down facing the fire. David Reece moved back. He said, "Right. Go on, Hull, tell him."

Still at the window, Rainer asked, "This hypnotism—using it, could you make someone forget something? An event? A period of time?"

Odd question, Jason thought. The actor might have been suspecting what had happened during the first Elsie Vanetti disappearance.

"Perhaps," he said. "Why?"

Rainer explained why. This was the idea. It was clever, Jason mused, and it would work.

"Just the past half hour or so," Rainer said. "Could you do it?"

"Yes. Easily."

"Would it take you long?"

"Ten minutes."

David Reece said, "Impossible."

"I can take longer if that'll make you any happier."

"It has to be done properly. We'll test her afterwards, ask her questions. Then get you to make her forget that bit. Understand?"

"Yes, I understand."

"Also," Reece said, "she saw this room a couple of days ago, when she tried to escape. Can you make her forget that as well?"

"Yes."

"Okay, then," Hull Rainer said. "Will you do it? It's the only way to save yourselves. Elsie will be out, she will have cleared us, and you—well, we'll keep you here for a while and then let you go when it's all blown over."

That, Jason knew, was a lie. It wouldn't have convinced a child. They couldn't afford to let him live, knowing he would talk—unless they were willing to risk his story being ignored in the face of not only their denials but also Elsie's. That he doubted. He would be killed. But Elsie would live.

Rainer asked, "Well?"

Jason nodded slowly. "Yes, I'll do it."

Three minutes later Elsie was sitting on a chair in front of him, hypnotised. Only one of those minutes had been used in putting her into a trance, so strong was the rapport between them.

"Elsie," Jason said. "You had a dream. It was vivid and seemed real. But there were silly things in it too, as there always are in dreams. Do you remember it?"

She frowned slightly. "I'm not sure."

"You were in a parlour, being chased, trying to escape from your guard, the man in the stocking mask."

Reece said, "She ran upstairs and shouted out of a window." Jason repeated that, adding, "The whole thing was a dream."

"Was it?"

"And there's another one. I'll remind you. Listen. You dreamt a friend of yours, Jason Galt, called out to you and then came into the room where you were being kept prisoner. He took you out to that same parlour. A man was there. He told in a trance how you had been kidnapped. Next, your husband came. There was a fight for possession of a shotgun. You and Jason Galt ran out. A motorcycle exploded."

It occurred to Jason how truly dreamlike and absurd all this sounded. He asked, "Are you following, Elsie?"

She was not frowning now. "Yes."

"You and Jason ran over a field. You were shot at. You went into trees. You were being chased. It was one of those nightmares. Hull came with a knife but you escaped and got to a car. There you were caught by Hull and the man. You were taken back to your prison. Later, Jason Galt was taken out, then you joined him in the parlour and sat on a chair. That's all."

"Was that a dream?" Elsie asked, frowning again.

"Yes, it was."

"Oh. What a shame."

"Why? It was a nightmare. Why is it a shame?"

Elsie said, "He told me he loved me."

Jason swayed forward and his body tensed. He saw Reece's gun give a warning jerk. Hull Rainer said, "Get on with it."

Jason forced his tension away, his emotion to dim. It was for Elsie's own good that he was again, as so often before, taking from her a wanted possession.

He said, "On your knee is a writing pad. In your right hand is a pencil. Write down your two dreams."

Hull Rainer interrupted with, "Every detail."

Jason said, "Every detail, Elsie. Leave nothing out. Names, faces, places, conversation. Describe everything. Now please start to write."

As Elsie bent over and shivered her right hand in the air above her knee, Jason leaned back. Hull had been clever once more, about those details. It might have helped. Also it would help, Jason thought, if he could come up with something to give Elsie to say that would incriminate Hull, bringing the police here and saving them both. But there was nothing he could think of which would not come out when she was tested afterwards. He watched Elsie sadly.

She finished her pseudo writing. Jason said, "Look at this. See me take the pad and set it on fire. See the flames? There, the paper's gone, burned. There's nothing left. The dreams have disappeared. Be sure of that." After a pause, he asked, "Did you have a dream, Elsie?"

"I've had lots of dreams."

"This was about trying to escape from a parlour, and another about you and Jason Galt being chased, shot at, caught. Have you dreamt anything like that?"

Elsie shook her head. "No."

Jason looked at the two men. "All right?"

Hull Rainer nodded. Reece, his eyes crafty, said, "Ask her about coming here from her flat. See if she remembers anything that could give us away."

Jason asked. What Elsie said about her abduction and imprisonment seemed to satisfy David Reece. He said, however, "This is bloody good, y'know. We can sew it up real tight."

Hull Rainer: "What d'you mean?"

"We can get her to tell the police something totally

different, leave ourselves as clean as rain. She can describe maybe a high room with bars on the window." He talked on, outlining possibilities.

Jason saw hope. Although Elsie would do as ordered, she would not be able to supply the minutiae the police would press for and expect—marks on walls and furniture, fixtures, patterns of rugs or wallpaper, designs of objects—all those details which should be fixed in her mind after days of nothing else to look at.

But Hull Rainer obviously realised this himself. He said, "No, too complicated. Let's stick as close to the truth as possible."

David Reece shrugged. "I suppose you're right. But let's give her a bit to fog the bastards. Tell her she knew she was near the river because she could hear boats, stuff like that, and there were three men, all dressed the same. We'll leave the rest as it is."

Rainer nodded. He said, "Go ahead, Galt." After Jason had given Elsie those instructions, the actor evidently had an idea of his own for embellishment. He asked:

"Could you get her to take orders from me?"

"Simple ones, yes. It's just a change in voice. She'd accept that."

"Good. We'll do that after the test."

David Reece said, "Okay, everybody upstairs. We'll use the second bedroom. She saw the other."

---

Galt was kneeling on the floor in the tiny hallway. As an extra precaution, his hands had been tied behind his back. Hull was standing over him, the barrel of the shotgun resting on the nape of his neck.

Both men were looking through a crack of space down the hinge side of the ajar door. Beyond, in the bedroom, were Elsie and David Reece.

Elsie lay on the bed, still entranced. She had a blanket spread across her lower body. Her head and shoulders were propped up on pillows. Reece sat facing her on the edge of the bed.

He called, "Right."

Jason Galt had told Elsie she would come awake when she heard the number five spoken. Now he said, "One, two, three, four, five."

Intently, his nervousness simmering but under control, Hull stared through the slim gap. He watched as Elsie opened her eyes, sighed, blinked, and then looked at David Reece in growing surprise.

He said, "Hello, Miss Vanetti. Just relax. You're safe now. I'm a doctor and this is my house. We're waiting for the police to come."

She smiled tentatively, disbelievingly. "I'm safe? Free?"

"Yes. Your husband paid the ransom and they let you go. Apparently they gave you a sleeping draft. They put you in a lonely spot in the country. Some children found you."

"I can't believe it," Elsie said happily, clasping her hands. "I'm out of that place at last. How wonderful."

"Please, Miss Vanetti. You must keep calm. That's an order. You've had an ordeal and I've just given you an injection. So please take it easy."

She smiled and composed herself. "Yes, Doctor."

It's working, Hull thought jubilantly.

David Reece said, "The police want me to ask you a few questions. All right?"

"Yes, of course."

"Right. Now, what's the last thing you remember?"

Hull frowned as Elsie, poised for speech, seemed to change her mind. She looked down. There was a long pause before she said, "I was in bed."

"What next?"

"Nothing," she said, looking up. "I was here."

"Fine. Where were you? This place you were in."

"I—I was in a house by the river. I could hear the sirens and other sounds of boats."

"And there was one man?"

"No," Elsie said. "There were three men. They all wore boilersuits and stocking masks. But there was one I saw more than the others. He brought me the food."

"Would you know him again? Or the others?"

"No, I'm afraid not."

"What about the room you were in. Can you describe it?"

"Oh, yes. I'll never forget the awful place."

Hull listened with satisfaction as his wife gave a detailed description of the basement room, which, on the million-to-one chance of the police ever coming here, could be made totally different and its outer door removed.

Reece asked more questions, probed exhaustively for flaws. There were none. Finally he said, "Now, Miss Vanetti, I want you to listen to a voice." He glanced back, toward the door.

Hull prodded with the shotgun. Jason Galt said, "Elsie, can you hear me?"

Her mouth sagged with bewilderment. "Yes, it's . . ."

"Just listen. First close your eyes."

She did so. Jason said, slowly, spacing the words, "Five, four, three, two, one."

Elsie's body relaxed. All expression went from her face. She was back in a light trance.

It seemed so incredibly simple that Hull had the momentary suspicion that Elsie and Galt were working a trick. Which would be impossible, he realised, since Elsie hadn't known about the idea.

"Get up," Hull ordered. When the hypnotist rose they went into the bedroom. Reece was grinning. "We're golden," he said.

Hull gave him the gun. "Yes, but there was some hesitation at the beginning. That's got to go."

"Our clever mate can fix it."

Hull turned to the hypnotist. "Make her answer questions promptly, whenever she hears them. Also tell her to say she was blindfolded and taken for a ride, a *short* ride in a car. Got it?"

Jason Galt said a flat, "Yes."

"Okay. Now do that, tell her to forget this doctor scene, and then put her under my control."

Some minutes later, while Reece was taking Galt back down to the cellar and locking him in, Hull went into the bedroom. He washed the blood from his brow, tidied himself and put on his disguise.

He wondered if it was as Reece had said, about Elsie having seen one of the bedrooms. But if it was what he suspected, it didn't matter because it would have been accomplished at gunpoint. Which would not be the case with Jason Galt and Elsie—if they had a future together.

Hull straightened his shoulders as he looked at himself in the mirror. He felt better now about the end of Galt.

He went into the bedroom, took the blanket off his wife and said, "Get up, please. Come with me." He got a satisfying sensation of power when Elsie obeyed meekly. Taking her arm he led her downstairs.

David Reece was in the parlour. He handed over a black scarf, saying, "I've had this a million years. Picked it up on a road once. It couldn't be traced. And here's her cardigan and coat."

Hull put the scarf in his pocket, helped Elsie into the other garments. "That's all?"

"That's it, Hull boy. The other thing I'll attend to when I've got the money."

Hull nodded. "See you later." He took Elsie outside, put her in the back of the Ford and told her to lie down, which she did, curling up on the seat. Should anyone glance inside the car, she would simply be a woman sleeping.

Hull got behind the wheel and drove off. As he left the yard, he saw David Reece crossing with his shovel to the corpse of the motorcycle. First, Hull thought, he must get the letter from Shank Place. He knew the house, had been there once with Elsie. There was no one else in the building, the street was quiet. There would be no problems.

Second, get rid of Elsie safely. The best thing would be a busy commercial district where he wouldn't be noticed among all the other people. But he would have to find a deserted spot in the middle of it. The supposed kidnappers were to release Elsie in the evening in Soho. The police wouldn't expect them to be stupid enough to do that, so there was no problem there either.

Third, take the Ford back to the parking lot. But doing that and getting over to the MGB would take time, which was of the essence. It would be better to be at home when the police came or telephoned to say Elsie had been found—and that would happen quickly. They would think it odd if he were out when her release was imminent.

Another factor occurred to Hull, turning now at The Jolly Miller crossroads. Fingerprints. Not only were his own prints on this car, but also those of David Reece, Elsie and Galt.

He thought it over carefully as he drove to and through Compton Pool. There was no time and no place to give the car a thorough wiping. So he would not return it to the cinema car park. He would leave it somewhere near the MGB, thus cutting that journey, and go back for it in a day or two, take it to a car-wash and have it cleaned, going over it again inside himself to be doubly sure.

The marvellous thing, Hull thought, was that none of this was really necessary. There would be nothing to connect him with the Ford. But it was pleasant to know that, should the slightest suspicion arise, he had blocked off all leads.

Hull's nervousness subsided as he drove. In the first London suburb, stopping at traffic lights, he was pleased to note that not one of the passers-by so much as glanced at the car, let alone its occupants. He made a turn and headed for Camden Town.

Soon he was approaching Shank Place. It was the next turning on the left. Hull began to slow. There was little traffic here, moving or otherwise. He passed a parked truck. A taxi stood opposite the mouth of Shank Place. A car was coming the—

Hull snapped a look back at the taxi. His heart gave a running trill of beats.

Despite the driver's low-pulled cap and the upturned collar of his topcoat, Hull recognised him. It was Detective-Sergeant Bart. He sat slouched over the wheel, his gaze intently directed into the dead-end street.

Hull speeded up. Drawing level with the cab he averted his face. He continued driving quickly until he had left the area behind.

Calming, he told himself the letter would have to wait. Obviously, the police suspected Jason Galt of being involved in the kidnapping. They were watching the house but would call that off once Elsie was found. The letter could be picked up tonight. It would all work out beautifully. When Galt disappeared, they'd be convinced. He would be the one they looked for.

But Hull shuddered at how close he had been to disaster. He put a hand to his brow and found it wet.

Hull drove through two more suburbs and then slowed in the next. Its centre was a busy shopping mall. He turned into a side street, saw an alley, went into it. At the far end he swung onto a street. There were a few strollers. He stopped, reversed to a spot near the alley, parked and waited. The strollers thinned to a pair of middle-aged women going the other way.

Hull got out quickly and opened the back door. He said, "Come on, Elsie." His wife got up at once. He took her arm and hurried her outside and walked her into the alley. It was still deserted.

Hull took Elsie into the recessed gateway he had seen on the way along. He stood her facing the solid gate. Bringing out the scarf he slipped it over her eyes and tied a rough knot.

He looked around. The way was still clear. He began to back off. Before turning and running, he said, "One, two, three, four, five."

---

There was something over her eyes. She supposed it was the blanket. But if so, why was she standing? And why was there a different smell, the scent of outdoors?

Elsie's hands, already on the way up to her face, touched a band of material, followed it around to the back, found a knot. She pushed up and took off the band.

A few inches in front of her was wood, painted green. It was alien to her experience. She whirled, afraid and unsteady, and overbalanced slightly so that she needed to steady herself against the brickwork at either side.

It's a dream, she told herself reassuringly.

But everything looked so real, so clear and defined. The wall and gates opposite, this brickwork, the cobblestones underfoot, a gutter drain in the middle.

Elsie lifted what she held. It was a black scarf, soft and silky, frayed at one edge. It was not hers. She had never seen it before. And, she realised, she was fully dressed, even to her topcoat.

This was ridiculous, Elsie thought, because it couldn't be a dream. One minute ago—less, one second ago—she had been in that room, in bed, naked, one hand tied to the post. Now she was dressed and outside. Ridiculous.

Still afraid, Elsie leaned forward and peered out beyond the two uprights of brickwork. She was in an alley. It was unknown to her. She stepped out and began to walk.

Slowly, her spirits started to climb and her fear to lessen. All this, she thought, could only mean the hoped and prayed for: that she was free. She had been released. A ransom had been payed and the gang had let her go.

But how had she got here? If one second she had been in bed, the next standing in an alley—well, how? A drug, perhaps. They had put something in her food. Or possibly she'd had another bout of amnesia. The same as last time. Except now she remembered everything, except getting here, which was unimportant.

It was all unimportant, Elsie thought. The only thing that mattered was freedom!

She smiled suddenly. She walked on at a faster pace and lifted her head. She could feel the sun on her face, smell the fresh air, hear her shoes smacking hard on solid stone.

She came onto a street. Left was quiet. To the right were people and shops and traffic. There was the marvel of bustle and noise. She went toward it at a stroll, savouringly.

A woman was coming this way. She looked at Elsie, glanced away and then looked back. She frowned, slowing, as Elsie passed and went on.

At the corner Elsie stopped to look behind. The woman, who had also halted, shook her head as if in dismissal of a foolish notion, turned and went on her way.

Elsie moved into the passing crowd. She continued to walk at a carefree stroll. She knew she should hurry to the nearest police station and let them know she was free, but there would, naturally, be hours of questioning—inside. She had been inside long enough. First she wanted to enjoy being out in the open.

Several people coming in the other direction stared at her. One stopped and made as though to speak. Elsie went on.

She reminded herself she must not tell the police she couldn't recall how she'd got here. That might cast doubt on everything else she could tell them about her imprisonment, and they had to believe what was useful in that in order for the gang to be caught.

More people were looking. Glancing aside, Elsie saw that other watchers were keeping abreast with her. She had been through this sort of thing before in the two months since her rebirth. Then it had been merely the interest of seeing a celebrity. Now it was something more.

Patently, it would not be long before someone decided that yes, this happy stroller was the kidnapped actress. She had better forget about her long outdoor amble.

On the other side of the street Elsie saw a patrolling constable, walking solemnly with hands afted. She moved to the kerb. The traffic passed close and fast. People jostled her on either side.

Traffic easing, Elsie ran across the road. She went to the policeman and stopped him with, "Excuse me, Officer."

"Yes, ma'am?" he asked, and then his face swiftly congealed from mechanical politeness to a stare. He said a soft, "Hey."

"I'm Elsie Vanetti."

"Jesus Christ. I mean—sorry—I mean—"

Elsie laughed. The policeman, a decade younger than herself looked to be torn among confusion at his response, shock at his find, and delight at what would be the consequences.

She asked, "Could you take me to the nearest police station, please?"

"Could I? Blimey, yes."

A crowd was gathering. The constable took Elsie's arm. "This way, ma'am. It's not far. Elsie Vanetti. Blimey."

Elsie was still smiling. It was wonderful to be happy, she mused, and to be making someone else happy. It was even nice to be giving excitement to the people who were trailing behind. And soon she would be seeing Jason. It seemed ages since they had been together, but it was only three or four days.

The constable asked, "How did you get here, ma'am?"

Without thinking, Elsie said, "They blindfolded me and put me in a car and took me for a short drive." She was surprised to hear herself say this. She supposed it could be true, must be, even though she couldn't remember it.

She added, "It's not very clear. I think I was a bit dazed, perhaps shocked."

"Before that," the constable asked. "What's the last thing you remember?"

"I was in bed," Elsie answered promptly. Again she was surprised. Also she was irked. She felt herself blushing. That was something she had not intended mentioning to anyone. She didn't want it known how close she had come to giving herself sexually in exchange for the promise of freedom.

And now Elsie wondered: Did I go through with it after all? Did we continue when the man came back from investigating that noise? Is that why I'm here, and why I can't remember anything beyond waiting for him?

One of the doctors who had treated Elsie for amnesia had

explained that fugue, as he called her condition, could be caused by the mind purposely blotting out an experience which was hated or traumatic.

That could well be the case here, Elsie thought. And if so, all the better. The barter having been honourable, she had nothing to berate herself for morally, and there were no unpleasant or disgusting memories to plaguingly return. And she was free.

Elsie pulled the constable's arm tight against her. "Let's hurry," she said.

———◆———

The street was residential and quiet. Huge sycamore trees canopied most of the roadway and kept light from the houses, which looked resentful, glum, like dusty umbrellas in a drought. There were cars parked with a carelessness of alignment which showed the street's lack of consequence as a traffic artery.

Hull drew the Ford into the side and stopped. He got out, locked up and set off walking. In glancing around as if admiring the trees, he saw no observer.

He pulled the muffler from about his neck, the movement casual, and put it away after he had rounded the first corner. At the next corner he did the same with his spectacles. At the next, he took off and pocketed the cap. The fourth corner he turned brought him to the church, and his MGB.

With a huge, grunting sigh of relief he got in. He drove away swiftly. Already, he thought, Elsie would be with the police.

Six minutes later Hull was turning into the mouth of the basement garage. He noted with satisfaction that the front of the apartment house was deserted.

He parked quickly, didn't bother to lock the car, strode to the service stairs and ran up. The coast was clear above, not that it mattered. He let himself into the flat. Its air of peace and security made him smile, and the smile made him realise he was nervous.

He went into his bedroom. In different parts of the clothes closet he put cap, muffler and jacket. He donned a tweed sports coat. In a drawer he put the spectacles and the keys for the rented Ford.

With impeccable timing, the telephone rang as Hull walked into the living room. He picked up the instrument and chanted his number. A brisk male voice asked, "Is that Mr. Hull Rainer?"

"Yes, it is," Hull said, acting. "But look, I want to keep this line open. I can't talk now. I'm expecting—"

"This is the police, sir. We have your wife."

"What? Where? How wonderful!"

"She's here at Canning Wood Police Station. She seems unharmed."

"Thank God for that," Hull said fervently. "I'll be right over. Many thanks. Goodbye." He chopped down the receiver.

Neat, he thought. Everything's neat. Not a thing to worry about.

He strode out of the flat and went to the elevator. It was on its way up. It stopped, the doors slid back, a neighbour couple came out.

Excitedly Hull told them as he brushed past, "Elsie's been found. She's safe. I'm going there now." He and the couple were still exclaiming at each other when the doors closed.

You're thorough, Albert, Hull told himself. Got to hand you that.

Below in the lobby, he was disappointed at not finding someone else he could act it up for. He went down one flight into the garage, got in the MGB and drove away.

Canning Wood Police Station was a glowering Victorian heap, soot-blackened and grim, like a museum of surgical errors. Aptly, the small crowd standing outside had a ghoulish air.

Three police cars were double-parked in the roadway. Hull joined the illegality. He entered the building at an eager stride.

The first person he saw, in what seemed a fifty-strong mob,

was Chief Inspector Harold Wilkinson. He came forward with outstretched hand and a kink at one corner of his mouth that was probably a smile.

He said, loudly to be heard above the noise, "Afternoon, sir."

"Good afternoon." They shook hands. "This is great news."

"Yes, sir. Let me get you out of this chaos. This way."

A minute later, Hull was sitting with Wilkinson at a bare table in a room whose only other furniture was a pair of chairs, and the policeman was saying:

"We'll see Miss Vanetti presently. I haven't seen her myself yet. The doctor's with her now. Just a check-up. She appears to be perfectly fine and you'll probably get the okay to take her home. It's been only a few days, after all."

"Seems like a lifetime to me. Thank God it's over."

Wilkinson nodded. He was leaning forward on the table, his unlit pipe cuddled in both hands. "Yes. And it takes the heat off you, Mr. Rainer."

"Me?" Hull asked, showing his surprise. "You suspected *me?*"

"At first, yes. But now Miss Vanetti's described the man who abducted her, and he was too big to be you. Before, you understand, we only had your description of him."

"I see," Hull said, feeling easy. "So I could have made it up. I could have been the man myself."

"Exactly, Mr. Rainer. And there were other irregularities we wondered about."

"Tell me, Inspector."

"Well, according to the detective who came in answer to your emergency call, the blood from your head wound was a vertical trickle. That could only have happened if you'd bled standing up, not lying flat out."

Hull got out his cigarettes. "Yes, that is odd. How could that've happened?"

"There's possibly a reasonable explanation. Maybe the blood only started with activity, once you became conscious and got up."

Hull lit a cigarette with steady hands. "I guess."

"And then there were your actions. Suspicious. You were doing a lot of coming and going, which might have been nothing, plus your insistence on a solo delivery of the money. Again, no one but you saw the collector."

"I imagine that's what the man wanted."

"Of course," Wilkinson said. "Anyway, it's all over now."

"A great relief to us all."

"By the way, you'll be happy to know that we'll be able to identify most of the ransom money when we get our hands on those boys."

Hull took a deep drag of smoke before asking, "How?"

"Serial numbers. You were followed when you went to your bank, after you'd left me in the store. I called the manager. I asked him to take the numbers down."

Hull shook his head. "He wouldn't have had the time."

"They were mostly new notes in wads. He only needed to note the first and last numbers in each wad."

"Yes, I see," Hull said. He felt queasy. "Yes, that should help quite a bit."

"We certainly hope so."

Hull told himself there was nothing to worry about. Quite the reverse, in fact. The money, both his and David Reece's, could easily be "washed," preferably somewhere abroad, and in such a way as to put suspicion on a mythical gang, or Galt on the run.

He said, smiling, "You didn't tell me I was under suspicion."

There was a tap on the door and a voice said, "Ready, sir."

Wilkinson got up. He said, "We wanted it that way. The confident man gets careless."

Also rising, Hull said, "Curiously enough, it never occurred to me for a moment that I was suspected."

"As you were innocent, sir, why should it?"

They left the room, went along a corridor and into another, where there followed a period of cheerful confusion, of greeting and congratulation and introduction. What pleased Hull most was the fact that Elsie didn't draw back from his embrace.

The group settled.

Hull sat with his wife on a couch of scuffed leather. On a chair nearby was a middle-aged man, the police surgeon, who smiled on his patient with a proprietary air. The same manner was worn by a young constable who stood by the door. At a desk facing the couch sat a policewoman stenographer. On the edge of that desk sat Inspector Wilkinson.

He looked at the middle-aged man. "Well now, what's the verdict?"

"Fit as a fiddle," the doctor said. "No need for hospitalisation. All quite normal. Fine state of health, in fact."

Wilkinson turned to Elsie. "You seem to have been well treated, ma'am."

She nodded. "I was really. I can't complain too much on that score."

"I take it, then, that you remember everything this time."

"Oh yes, Inspector. Every detail."

"Good," Wilkinson said. "So let's start with the place. Where were you?"

"In a house by the river. I knew that because of the sound of boats, sirens and so on, although I didn't see anything when I was put . . ."

Elsie talked on. Hull listened with a glow of satisfaction. He told himself his idea had been brilliant.

Chief Inspector Wilkinson was particular. He asked about temperature, the make of electric fire, detailed descriptions of not only objects but the food which had been served. Elsie answered promptly and volubly.

"Now, who exactly did you see, Miss Vanetti?"

"There were three men," Elsie said. "They all wore the same boilersuits, hats and stocking masks. The one I saw most, who brought the food, was the one who took me away from home. He was about six feet tall and had a gruff voice."

"We'll come back to that later, ma'am. How did you get here?"

"I was blindfolded and put in a car and taken for a short ride."

"That's all?"

"Yes. The next thing I knew, I was alone and pulling off the scarf. This is it."

Wilkinson took the piece of black material and described it for the benefit of the stenographer, who was writing busily. He put the scarf in his pocket and said:

"Getting back to the main thug, Miss Vanetti. Could he possibly have been Jason Galt?"

Elsie straightened and blinked with surprise. She looked at Hull and then back at Wilkinson. "Jason? Why, no. That's silly."

"Perhaps not, ma'am. He was tall, you didn't see his face, he could have disguised his voice."

"But surely," Elsie said, frowning, "surely you don't suspect Jason of being involved. How could you?"

"Quite easily, ma'am. Since the abduction he's been acting oddly. We kept an eye on him sporadically, and have watched his house full time since the ransom demand was received by your husband—I only called the watch off a while ago, when I was told you had been found."

Hearing that, Hull had to stop himself from smiling.

Elsie said, "But this is ridiculous. Jason? No, I don't believe it."

"I'm not saying it's definite, Miss Vanetti. Only that it's a possibility. And he has been acting strangely. He's stayed away from his work, he hired a motorcycle, and at the time of the ransom collection he wasn't at home."

"He might have been searching for me."

"Might have, yes. But one man abducted you, one man picked up the money. The whole thing, you see, could be a one-man job."

Elsie shook her head. "There were three."

Wilkinson was looking at her thoughtfully. He asked, "Isn't it possible that Galt hypnotised you and made you say that?"

"Absolutely not, Inspector. And the main thug, in no way could he be Jason. I know Jason very well."

Wilkinson nodded. "Okay. Let's get back to that room."

The questioning went on. Elsie answered without hesitation. She was doing beautifully, Hull thought, as was Wilkinson with his suspicions of Jason Galt.

Patting his wife's hand from time to time, Hull kept up an attitude of concern and interest.

At last Elsie said, "Inspector, you've already asked me that question twice."

He made a gesture of apology. "Sorry, Miss Vanetti. And you're right, we have done enough for today. You'll want to be getting home now, of course."

"Of course," Hull said.

Chief Inspector Wilkinson pushed himself up from the desk. "Perhaps I could ask you to come to Scotland Yard tomorrow, ma'am. There'll be a formal statement for you to sign."

Elsie said, "Be glad to."

"Also I'd like you to talk to our linguistics chap. Whatever you can tell him about your guard's speech patterns might be useful. Shall we say about noon?"

"I'll be there," Elsie said. She and Hull rose. They shook hands with Wilkinson, next with the doctor. They were moving toward the young constable when the door beside him opened. In came Detective-Sergeant Bart.

Wilkinson said, "Better late than never."

The tall, sad-eyed policeman said, "Sorry about that."

"Where were you?"

It was Elsie who answered. She said, "I was in a house by the river."

---

A short, awkward silence followed. Elsie felt slightly embarrassed. Everyone glanced at her, and she noted that Hull seemed more put out than herself; the polite expression on his face had become tight.

She mumbled, "Excuse me."

Detective-Sergeant Bart said, "That old taxi broke down."

Wilkinson nodded. "It's not the the first time. It should've been retired years ago."

"Right, sir."

"So how did you get here?"

Before Bart could reply, Elsie said a prompt, "I was blindfolded and put in a car and taken for a short ride."

This time the following silence was less short, more awkward, while Elsie's embarrassment was more acute. She blushed. She couldn't imagine what was making her be so foolish.

Everyone was looking at her; not glancing—looking. Hull had drawn away, almost as though he were trying to disassociate himself from her silliness. He stood with his back to the wall.

Inspector Wilkinson had wrinkles in his brow. He turned back to face Bart, asking, "Yes?"

"Well, I left it and got a real taxi."

"Okay. And what about Galt?"

Detective-Sergeant Bart said, "He hasn't been seen since early this morning. He could be in there, I suppose. Could've got in another way, after returning the bike."

"That's all you have to report?"

"Yes, sir."

"Callers?" the inspector asked. "Did you see anyone?"

Elsie said, "I saw three men. They—" She broke off in a returning surge of embarrassment. She went on, "Sorry. I don't know what's wrong with me. I won't interrupt again." But she was astonished to hear herself say:

"They were all in boilersuits, hats and masks."

In a voice which seemed to some from a long way off, Hull said, "Darling, we'd better go. Please."

She nodded and made to move away.

"One moment," Wilkinson said. "One moment, ma'am. I want to ask the doctor a question." He turned. "Tell me, Doctor, where were you?"

27

The man looked back blankly at the inspector while Elsie heard herself saying, "I was in a house by the river. I could hear . . ." She clamped a hand over her mouth, and against her fingers finished, ". . . the sirens and other boat noises."

Wilkinson turned quickly. "Bart," he said. "Go at once to Jason Galt's house. If he doesn't answer, break in."

Bart strode out of the room.

More bewildered now than embarrassed, Elsie gazed around at the others, trying to understand. The doctor, the constable and the stenographer looked equally uncomprehending. Hull, Elsie saw with a start, seemed stricken. Hands flat against the wall, he was staring with a teeth-bared expression of terror at Inspector Wilkinson; which was ridiculous, Elsie thought, because all the inspector was doing was smiling broadly.